# DOLPHIN GIRL

## SHEL DELISLE

ISBN:  0615554458
ISBN-13: 978-0615554457

# DEDICATION

For my favorite pod mates
Ken, Matt, Cam and Ryan

Shel Delisle

# CHAPTER ONE

I never knew how painful this would be.

That's what I was thinking—what I was about to say aloud to Lexie—when Tattoo Man asks, "How come a dolphin?"

"What?"

"Everyone comes in here with a reason for why they get inked, and everyone has a reason for what they pick." He harrumphs at himself while the needle pricks the skin on my lower back. Tears flash, blurring my vision. "You should tell me. It'll take your mind off the hurt."

From my awkward belly-down position on this imitation dentist chair, I catch glimpses of Tattoo Man's arms and hands. If this wasn't just another steamy day in South Florida, you'd swear he was wearing a long-sleeved shirt. But he's not. It's his tats, solid from shoulder to fingertips.

Lexie and Desiree—my partners in crime—wait for me,

sitting along the wall in metal chairs with shredded black leather seats. Lexie rests the back of her hand against her mouth, and I can't figure out if she's holding back a laugh or a shriek of utter horror. Desiree's flipping through some magazine. *Organic Gardening*, or something like that.

"Every picture tells a story, don't it?" Tattoo Man sings.

"Huh?"

"Rod Stewart. You know him, right?"

I have no idea what he's talking about. "How much longer?" I ask.

"A little bit. You might as well tell me why a dolphin. Unless you like it when I sing you oldies."

Not especially. "Okay. Why a dolphin? I think the whole thing comes from this time when I was around five years old."

"You're eighteen now?"

*Sixteen.* "Yeah."

And so I tell Tattoo Man the story of when our next-door neighbors at the time—the Mitchells—bought a third-hand boat and invited us to go for a cruise. The strangest thing is my almost total recall of that day. The way the wood dock creaked as we walked toward their boat. The strips of space between the boards, where I could see and smell the salt water below. I remember feeling afraid that my sandals might catch on the edge of one of those boards and I would fall through the crevice.

The gaps were way too small for that to happen, probably

only three or four inches wide, but I worried about it anyway. Apparently, so did my mom.

"Careful, Jane!" she said, gripping my wrist as tightly as a knotted shoelace.

At the boat, Mr. Mitchell lifted me up and over onto the deck. He handed Mom an orange life vest.

"Here you go." She wrestled it over my head. It smelled wet and a little dusty, like it had been buried somewhere. "This will keep you safe." Mom emphasized every word as she pulled the straps taut.

The back of the jacket had this huge cushion roll that kept my head immobile and made it practically impossible to look around without turning my whole body. "Take it off," I begged. "It's uncomfortable."

"It's for your protection. In case you fall in the water."

"John isn't wearing one," I complained.

"John's almost eight."

"I won't get hurt. I'm a good swimmer." Which was 100% true. I'd taken swim lessons the summer before, and the instructor had called me a little fish.

Suddenly, the needle stings and Tattoo Man says, "So you want a dolphin 'cause you're a good swimmer. Makes sense."

"No," I say, "there's more to the story."

"There always is."

"Well, really, there was no use arguing with my mom about

the life vest."

Because it was not coming off, no matter how much I yanked at it or made faces or hurky-jerked around like I was being tortured. So I finally sank into one of the seats and decided to make the best of it.

After all, the sun was shining and once we'd pulled out of the marina, Mr. Mitchell sped up. A clean breeze blew into my face, whipping my long hair behind me. The only thing that could have made it better would've been convincing Mom to take the life jacket off. Or, at least, loosen it a little.

Finally we made our way out of the Intracoastal.

"Let's open her up." Mr. Mitchell pushed the throttle forward, and we took off, skimming along waves.

Even eleven years later in this sterile tattoo parlor, I can smell the gasoline, salt water and seaweed. I can still feel the wind blowing in my face. I can practically taste the spray that landed on my lips. It's weird to remember every single detail, every single sensation after so much time has passed.

Eventually, when we were a ways offshore, Mr. Mitchell cut the engine. "Look there." He pointed at a spot we'd just gone past. All I could see was the sun reflecting off the waves as the boat rocked back and forth, but Mr. Mitchell didn't lower his arm. "C'mere, Jane." He pulled me over to him and let me follow along the site line of his finger. "See them?"

I didn't know what he was talking about. And then, a fin

broke the surface of the water.

"Is that a shark?" I asked. I knew all about sharks because John had played for a baseball team that had one as their mascot. But even as I asked this question, I knew it was definitely not a shark. The shape rolled forward until there was only a hint of its tail.

Mr. Mitchell's finger tracked one as it resurfaced. "A dolphin. I'd guess a bottlenose. Keep watching, you'll probably see the others."

I did. They surged alongside the boat and then swam to the front of it. Mr. Mitchell and Dad took me up there to get a closer look.

"Make sure you have a good hold on her, Tom." Mom's voice was as tight as my life vest.

The next thing I knew, I was hanging over the edge while two of the dolphins grinned up at me. "Hi there, dolphins," I said.

"To this day," I tell Tattoo Man, "I swear they said, 'C'mon in and play. The water's nice.' They didn't say it with their mouths, but it's like I heard their voices in my mind. And so I wiggled out of my Dad's arms and jumped."

Tattoo Man stops with the needle. "That was either really brave or really stupid."

"They bobbed around me and nudged me gently with their noses while my mom screamed in the background, 'Get her in the boat! Get her in the boat!'"

Everything happening on the boat seemed like chaos, while my spot in the water seemed calm beyond description. It's almost like I was separated from the boat by more than just a few feet. It felt like I was in another world, another place.

In the middle of all of this, there was a huge splash next to me. Mr. Mitchell was in the water. 'Stay with us' came from the dolphins. And I would have, if two strong hands didn't grab me and lift me overhead into my dad's arms.

"Are you okay Jane?" He set me down onto the deck.

"It was neat, Daddy." I tried to walk over to the edge of the boat to look at the dolphins again, but my mom had knelt next to me. She grabbed me by both shoulders and shook me while looking into my eyes. "You could've gotten hurt. You could've drowned. What made you do that?"

"The dolphins talked to me. They said for me to come in."

Mom shook her head, locking her frantic eyes on mine. "Don't you ever do that again. You almost gave me a heart attack. Not ever. Do you hear me?"

I laugh, remembering Mom's look. "I was never, not even a little bit, in danger," I tell Tattoo Man.

"I 'spect you're right." He wipes the tip of the needle with a paper towel. "You're all done."

I'm not sure if he means with my story or the tattoo, but then he angles a mirror.

I crane my neck to see my body art. "I love it."

"Glad to hear that. And that was some story you told me. Now I know why you're getting inked in addition to why you picked a dolphin."

He knows why I'm doing this? Honestly, I'm not even sure I know why I wanted a tattoo badly enough to fake being eighteen. "You could tell all that from my story?"

"Sure."

"So why am getting it?"

"Because—" he sits back to admire his work— "it's your way of ripping off that life jacket."

*Scientists and trainers often observe signs of intelligence in dolphins. One of the most remarkable traits is that dolphins recognize themselves in a mirror, proving they have self-awareness.*

*(Excerpt:* The Magic and Mystery of Dolphins*)*

# CHAPTER TWO

I peer out at myself in the mirror through the mouth of my Halloween costume. The transformation is complete. I am Dolphin Girl.

Wild.

Graceful.

Free.

Okay, so my life is actually nothing like that, but the costume lets me pretend otherwise.

Sheathed in a leotard made from a sleek, silvery material, I move my flipper-arms, the pectoral fins, to see how I'll look dancing. Cool. The dorsal fin on my back bounces a bit but should stay attached if I don't dance too crazy.

I shouldn't be playing around in my costume because I haven't completed Mom's totally boring, totally anal and incredibly long list of housekeeping tasks, which hangs on the refrigerator with a Do Not Ignore magnet. Here's what I can't ignore.

Today, Item #6—clean the bathroom grout—is what sent me running for sanctuary. She makes me crazy.

I scrutinize the costume's reflection. The oversized head is cartoonish, like a college mascot, only girly with an oversized pink bow and long eyelashes. I'm not sure why I made a Disney version of a dolphin. Maybe this way, if it's completely uncool, I can pass it off as a joke?

But it's not, because the hours I spent constructing the costume are too immense to count, and I'm happy with the results even if others aren't—namely, Mom.

The first time she saw it she had a conniption. "Jane, what in the world? Why don't you dress up as a cute black cat or a witch?"

So tame. So lame. So Mom.

"It's cool, dontcha think?" I knew she didn't but tried to convince her anyway.

Mom struggled to drag my dad from the sports page. "Tom, did you see Jane's costume for her Halloween dance? Don't you think she should go as something more—" her shoulders heaved as she searched for the right word before sighing—"normal?"

Dad mumbled and hummed behind the newspaper until my mom tapped her fingernail on the page and peeled it down. "Tom. Do you agree with me?"

"I really don't care what she goes as." My dad lifted the paper. "When has Jane ever been normal? What makes you think she's going to start now?"

And that summed up exactly how my dad felt about me and everything else. Apathetic. But I still couldn't believe he said it with me in the room. Nose to newspaper, maybe he didn't even realize I stood five feet away. But those five feet may as well have been half the world.

I guess I should've been used to it. Most days I'm convinced God made a mistake when he put me in this family.

It can happen, y'know—He makes mistakes. Just look at the duckbill platypus.

Grabbing fish food from my drawer, I head to the oversized tank in the corner by my desk. Flipper, my goldfish, is the only acceptable family pet because he doesn't shed or bark and only uses the bathroom in his tank. He swims to the surface, and I sprinkle a few flakes and make kissy noises.

"Do you like my costume?" I ask him.

He darts, snatching the flakes. I take this as a yes.

Even though I love the costume and Flipper has given it a fins up, a voice of self-doubt bubbles to the surface. What will everyone think? Will anyone want to dance with me? Do I have the guts to wear this?

It's funny. I knew Mom and Dad wouldn't love this look, but if I'm honest with myself, I want someone to like it.

There's a knock on the door, and Mom sticks her head in. "Jane." Except the way she says my name makes me feel I've been caught doing something wrong. Ordinarily she waits for an answer, but not this time. She takes one look at me. "Again with the dolphin thing?" She shakes her head and blurts, "Did you finish the grout?"

I didn't even start. "Um, no."

Mom eyes me and walks over to my closet, throwing her hands up. She pulls tops still on their hangers from the bar and tosses them into a pile on my bed, covering my ripple-patterned comforter. I picked the comforter, colored in every shade of blue from deepest midnight to palest aqua, because it looked ocean-y.

"Would you take that off? It's ridiculous and uh, uh...a distraction."

The head is warm, so I pull it off and set it on my bed next to a pile of clean clothes and a worn copy of *The Magic and Mystery of Dolphins*. Then I step carefully out of my costume and lay it on the bed. Mom brushes it aside.

With my back to her, I hear, "Dear God! What is *that?*"

"Huh?" *Oh, crap.*

"That bandage. Did you get hurt?"

"It's nothing."

"That's not 'nothing.'" Mom's voice is worried as she walks toward me. "That bandage is big. Are you okay? Let me see what happened."

This is what happened. I've been caught. Big time. And it's way worse than not getting the grout done.

As Mom peels the bandage off, I gasp. Then she does too. "Please tell me that is not a tattoo on your waist. Please." The worry is replaced with irritation.

My answer is silence. I wish I had a good lie handy.

"My God! What were you thinking? What possessed you!" Her mouth opens and closes like a fish out of water. She's going into shock as she plops onto my bed. "That's illegal, Jane. You're not eighteen. How did you?"

Leave it to her to think of that. "Mom," I start with a calm voice. "A lot of kids get them before they turn eighteen."

"They are not my kids!" she practically yells. "And how? Tell me, how do they get them if it's illegal?"

I don't even breathe.

"How did you get one?" Her voice is several decibels louder.

I don't think I should tell her about my fake ID or how Desiree helped me, or how Lexie drove. It's what you would call TMI. "It's not a big deal, Mom."

She grabs a handful of tops off my bed and re-hangs them

in the closet, sorting them by sleeve length and color. Uh-oh. She always does this when she's going nuke. "Oh no, Jane. You're wrong. This is a very big deal."

"Look. It's so little."

"You'll never get a job with one of those."

"Mom! Who's going to look at my back during a job interview? I don't think you'd want me interviewing for any jobs where my back—"

"Don't you get smart with me! It'll turn colors and stretch out as you get older. Believe me, you're going to regret this." She's got the cleaning mads. Once all the shirts are in the closet, she moves to my neon corkboard, hand-cut to resemble a coral reef. The reef is stuck with pushpins holding hundreds of my sketches, poems and paintings. "What a mess," She pulls out pushpins, making a pile on the desk. "Why don't you just frame a few of these? It would look so much neater."

"Mom," I plead. Her hands fly between the corkboard and the desk, pulling down all my work.

She glares at me colder than today's frozen casserole. Which was Item #3 on today's list. The casserole, I mean, not the glare.

"You're grounded. One month. I want you straight home after school. Do your homework and the list. That's it, nothing else."

No way. Not now! "One month is kinda long, dontcha think?"

"A month isn't long enough. I'm so mad right now, Jane, I could ground you 'til you graduate. How could you do this? Your brother never did anything like this—" She pauses for five beats— "in high school."

"John skipped school, and you didn't even ground him."

"That was different. He asked our *permission* to skip. It was senior skip day. He was a *senior*, Jane." She taps the top of my dresser with her manicured nail. "Totally different." She taps once more. "Besides, considering how things have turned out, maybe we should've done things differently with John. I don't want you ending up like him."

The whole John/Desiree thing bugs her so much. Now I have to pay for it.

"It starts after the dance, right?"

"It starts now." Mom jabs a pushpin in my direction for emphasis. She's not close enough to do any real damage with it.

"My costume. The decorations. I've worked so hard on them."

While she takes apart my reef, I sit on the corner of my bed, the only spot not covered with clothes. I glance at the mural-sized dolphin poster hanging on the opposite wall. The poster was a compromise. I wanted to paint an underwater mural, but Mom said no way, that it'd be impossible to paint over when I moved out. I guess she can't wait.

A tear slips from my eye. I brush it away. Even if it'd help my cause—and as angry as Mom is right now, it probably wouldn't—I don't want her to see me cry.

Is there any chance at all that I can get her to postpone the grounding? It kills me that I might miss the dance.

Not likely. She hasn't stopped sorting and categorizing since she saw my dolphin. Now skirts hang on the left, pants on the right.

"You know something, Jane. It'd be much easier for you to keep your closet organized if you limited yourself to a few color combinations."

*Like beige, Mom?*

She's got rules, schedules and lists for everything. What you should wear to the Halloween dance—black cat or witch. Or when to bake the stroganoff—4:45 p.m. today in a 350-degree oven. Or how a house should be decorated and kept—varying shades of beige with every little thing in its place.

"This is so unfair," I shout. If we were any place else in the house, I would stomp to my bedroom and slam the door.

Mom holds an armful of dirty clothes and bangs her forehead on the small wooden guitar that hangs off my eighth grade mobile. When Lexie started the Ginger Girls that year, she let me try every instrument but eventually decided I should stay involved by writing lyrics or designing cover art only.

Eleven brightly colored mobiles hang from the ceiling like jellyfish, each one marking a year of my life. In kindergarten, our teacher had us make them as a year-long project. When I brought it home, Mom hung it and said, "What a cute idea. You should do one for first grade, too."

I'm pretty sure she didn't realize I'd still be making and hanging them in eleventh grade.

"Stupid mobile," she says. "Let's take them down."

"Noooo," I wail. "Haven't you already punished me enough?"

She rubs the deep red mark on her forehead. "I'm sorry if you think I'm being too harsh. But you can't do whatever you want, whenever you want. You're only sixteen, and I'm the grown-up."

The thought of being more hemmed in than I already am is enough to give me hives. "What about the decorations for the dance?" I ask. "We haven't finished them yet, and they're counting on me."

Even with her back to me, I can tell she takes a huge breath. She spins around and puts her hands on her hips. "Can you finish during your lunch hour?"

"No. We work on them in the cafeteria." Even if I could get permission to work in the art room, I can't bear the thought of coming straight home from school. It's already a prison without that.

"Well, I suppose it's not fair to punish others, so you can finish. But if you finish Monday, grounding starts Tuesday. Am I clear? Don't think I won't know when your project is done. I will."

"Okay, okay, all right. I get it."

She turns away from me to face the closet.

"Sorry," I say.

Mom doesn't look at me but instead surveys her handiwork as she wipes her hands. "There, that's better."

My closet looks like Martha Stewart invaded and gave it a makeover. In a way, that's exactly what happened.

"Anything else I need to know?"

Head down, I say, "I started the stroganoff fifteen minutes late."

She sighs, like 'it figures,' and leaves.

You know what? Since I got home from getting inked, my day has turned into a huge suck tablet. There's no way I can swallow *this* pill. Mom's list. Then, she found out about my tattoo—I knew she would eventually—and now I'm grounded, no Halloween dance. I choke it all down as I re-tack a few sketches to the corkboard.

Dolphin Girl still lies on my bed, so I slip her onto a hanger and put her in my closet. I pull out a blue tee and stick it next to an orange sweatshirt. Then I move a purple skirt next to a lime green top. I wipe my hands.

There—that's better.

*Bottlenose dolphins have a unique way of introducing themselves. Each dolphin has its own signature whistle, which seems to be like the human version of a name. Upon encountering another dolphin, it will give its signature whistle, which is often repeated back. Perhaps this is a way of showing they recognize the whistler, or it could also be a welcome. Having a whistle seems important to being a part of dolphin social groups.*

*(Excerpt:* The Magic and Mystery of Dolphins*)*

# CHAPTER THREE

Whoever said "a man is judged by the company he keeps" must have spent some time in the main hall of Western Everglades High. Most of us, me included, cluster into pods like dolphins. Inside my pod, everyone is friendly with each other. Helpful. Supportive. At the same time, we keep our distance from others and, not surprisingly, some pods have more power—a sort of social pecking order. It's all very Darwinian.

As I pass the group who hangs at the front courtyard, I wave to Nigel Chang. He's wearing a psychedelic T-shirt with the face of his hero, Bob Marley.

Funny story. Last year in Spanish, Nigel complained to me,

"Y'know, I'm over the whole stoned Jamaican stereotype." The scent of weed rolled off of him.

"Then why don't you wait 'til after lunch to fire up?" I said.

He just laughed at me, but maybe he's taking my advice after all, since I don't smell any ganja wafting from their vicinity this morning.

"*¿Como esta*, Jane?" he yells over the head of one of his friends, flipping his long black bangs away from his face. Nigel grins from ear to ear—he always does, which of course makes him look more stoned. Even when he's not.

"Pretty good," is all I say. I'd like to stop, chat, see how he's doing, but instead I keep walking. No inter-pod mingling allowed.

Once inside, I turn left at the main hall. On the right is the science lab pod, the super smart, semi-nerdy kids who do very little other than study and occasionally join a group like Mu Alpha Theta or the Chess Club. I nod at Brendon/Brandon, a friend of Lexie's I sort of know, except for the fact that I can never remember his name.

Then I cruise past the bulletin board, where the involved students hang out. The SGA kids, the yearbook kids, the most-likely-to-succeed kids. Jordan Wilson, our class president, is pinning an announcement to the board, which is, I guess, how they ended up in this spot. Karen Perry says hi to me, and I "hey" back. After school, she and I have been working on the

23

decorations for the Monster Mash, this year's Halloween dance. I like her, even though we don't really hang together.

Up ahead I see Lexie, my best friend since second grade, and the rest of my friends, who circle the water fountain. It's especially appropriate I hang there with my whole dolphin obsession. Desiree thinks I might be reincarnated from one. Who knows? Could be.

My pod tends to go with the flow. We're smart, but not ultra-smart, like the science lab kids. We're attractive, but less shiny than our trophy-case classmates. Take me, for example. People always tell me I look like Hilary Swank, which is okay, I guess. But I hope it's more the *P.S. I Love You* Hilary than the *Boys Don't Cry* one. Either way, I'm no beauty queen. That would make me a Trophy-Caser.

Lexie squeals as I walk up. "Show them, show them, show them!" Her pale, punky hair has a small aqua streak today.

I smile. "Oh, you mean my felony. Wait a sec. I have some sketches for you. Band stuff."

I haul a sketchbook out of my backpack and flip to the middle, where I've dog-eared pages of drawings Lexie could use as the cover art for her CD. Most of the time she's laid back, but when it comes to the band she gets finicky. So even though she wants to use my art for their cover, it's gonna have to be the bomb.

The drawings are sketched large enough to give her an idea

of how the finished piece would look. When she picks one, I'll paint it in acrylic on an oversized canvas. Still, she's not gonna decide today because she's wants to rename the band. Tara convinced her that Ginger Girls sounds too annoyingly teenybopper.

"I like this one." Lexie points to a drawing of an indigo ocean with a full moon reflected on it. The sky is eerie, but the ocean underneath has a tranquil feel. "If we go with Estrogen Ocean, it's perfect." Even though I'm all about the ocean, I'm not a fan of that as the new name.

There's a group of people looking over Lexie's shoulders. I nod and as I flip the page my hand twitches a little, my shoulders tense.

"Oooooh." Lexie likes the abstract butterfly that's my favorite, too.

Artistically speaking, my biggest problem is that my lines are sometimes too tight—wonder where I get that from—but in this drawing, the lines are loose and rough and bold.

"What made you draw this? I hadn't really thought of a butterfly name," she says.

I shrug. "I don't know. I just felt like it."

"I love it!" Willow, another member of the band, gushes.

As I flip the page, I catch a glimpse of my cx-other-bestie, Alana, hanging out in front of the trophy case. She's practically eclipsed by that guy who's super tall with dark hair.

What's his name? I should know this. He's in English and Bio with me. It's something kinda different. Not Matt, or Josh, or Alex. He's incredibly gangly, except for these super-broad shoulders. Alana smirks at my pod and then whispers something to the guy.

The whole ex-bestie thing is pretty sad. She and Lexie and I were a real trio all through middle school and freshman year. Last year she started changing and then over the summer, Ashley Grant moved in across the street from her. The first day of school, when Travis spied beautiful Ashley, he offered her a spot by the case. Ashley dragged her new friend Alana along. Now she thinks she's too cool for us, and it definitely feels like there's more than twenty-five feet of hallway between us.

"Wow, that one is awesome," Lucas says as he throws an arm over Lexie's shoulder.

Lexie shakes her head. "It is, but I don't know—it doesn't feel quite right."

The sketch they're talking about is done from a dolphin's point of view. Underwater, looking up at a translucent jellyfish bobbing near the surface. While it's cool it doesn't go with Lexie's music.

"You're right. It's just what came to mind. That's it for now."

"Cool. So let me figure out a few things, and then I'll pick one." Then Lexie gets a fat smile and hollers, "Hey, everyone!

Thanks for comin' out tonight." Tara giggles and claps while heads from the other pods bob in our direction. "We've got a big announcement for all our fans," she continues in the same mic voice, and it's only one second before I realize what she's up to. "Our number-one fan and artist-in-residence Jane Robinson has some new artwork. It's not on her sketchpad, it's on her—"

Ohgod, ohgod.

"Whatd'ya call that?" my best friend asks quietly, and Lucas replies, "Spleen?"

Lexie hollers, "It's on her spleen."

We probably coulda used some help from the science pod on that.

"So, let's give it up for Jane's tattoo!" Lexie starts clapping, and my friends crack up and join the applause from a few other kids scattered through the front hall. I spy Nigel laughing. He couldn't have come inside for this.

When Tara yells "Show it!" I realize slinking away is out of the question, so I lift the back of my shirt and reveal the dolphin.

"Awesome!" Willow proclaims.

"Love it!" says Tara.

And then a snotty voice. "Omigod! She got a tramp stamp!" The voice is Alana's, and I wish I could sink into the floor. She's standing right behind me, holding onto the arm of the tall gangly guy she dragged over for my big reveal. "Were you on a hunt? Please tell me you at least got points for defacing your back." She laughs all cackly witch.

The tall guy doesn't laugh along with her. His eyes are glued to my lower back and then lift to meet mine. They flicker, and he smiles. Not cruelly, without one speck of judgment.

My face flushes. Who is he?

"Cool," he says. It's barely audible, but I heard it.

Alana's head snaps, and she quickly drags him away from the crowd that's checking out my tattoo. Seems like she heard him too. I wish for the bazillionth time I was better at remembering names. I know I'm supposed to know who he is, but I don't, and walking over to the trophy case to find out is completely off-limits as one of the unwritten rules of high school pods.

~~~

At lunch, I sit in the cafeteria, eating my tuna fish sandwich, minding my own business. I'm a little bit of a loner but not usually completely alone. But somehow I ended up in a lunch hour with freshmen. Last year, I ate with Lexie and the rest of my pod, but this year they're in third lunch with all the other juniors.

"Hey, Dolphin Girl, don't I know you?"

I swallow my tuna with a gulp and look up at the tall guy from the main hall. "My name is Jane," I say, which is a lot more direct than I wanted to be. Rude too.

He smiles. "I know," he says. "We have a couple of classes together."

Nice teeth on that guy—straight, white, and the best part is a small chip in one of his front ones. It makes him look friendly. And cute. I wish I could remember his name.

"Are we the only juniors in this period?" he asks.

"Might be." I move my backpack off the chair next to me onto the floor.

"I'll sit over there." He points to the spot across from me and saunters around the end of the table with his tray. I heave my backpack onto the chair.

When he sits, I check him out. Long nose, brown eyes, dark brown hair and that adorable chipped tooth. "What sport do you play?" I ask in the lamest attempt ever to be friendly.

"How do you know I play a sport?"

"You hang by the trophy case in the morning, right?"

"Yeah. So?"

"So everyone there is a jock. C'mon. Let me guess. Baseball? No, football, right?"

He laughs and confesses, "I'm a swimmer. Is that okay?"

Now, that *is* interesting. "Yeah. Sure. My brother's a jock. I'm sort of used to it."

He snorts. It's a dorky way to laugh, but I like it.

I push a few potato chips around with my tuna sandwich.

His tray is piled with three double cheeseburgers and two slices of pizza. He also has two apples and four cartons of milk. I tip my chin at his food. "When's the last time you ate?"

He snorts again. "I burn a lot of calories."

"Remind me to keep my body parts away from your mouth." I mean this as a joke about his appetite, but once it's out I realize how it sounds. I feel heat rise to my cheeks and know they're bright pink.

He raises one eyebrow. "I could forget."

My face blisters. What's hotter than hot pink?

It's a stroke of luck that saves me from a complete meltdown. A peach-fuzzed kid yells, "Hey Sam!" from a couple of tables over, and my lunch partner—*Sam*—*heys* back.

"He's on the swim team with me," Sam explains before he polishes off burger number two.

"You're Sam," I say in a way that declares I'm partially brain-dead.

"You didn't even know my name?"

"Don't take it personally," I apologize. "I'm atrocious with names."

I try not to stare at him while he devours the rest of his food. It's surprising, given the situation, that I'm not completely uneasy. It's a new person—a *guy* person—from the trophy case pod no less, and I still feel mostly comfortable.

He chugs a carton of milk and scrunches the container flat.

There's one awkward moment of silence until he asks, "Wanna play a game?"

It sounded a little weird, but so what, I'm a little weird. "What's the game?"

Sam, hands folded, grows serious. "What if Dolly Parton married Derek Mee?"

Derek Mee is the smartest kid in the senior class and a leading member of the science lab pod. Also, he's borderline nerdy.

I crack up. "I have no idea."

"She'd be Dolly Parton Mee." Sam snorts.

I laugh again. "Where'd you hear that?"

"I make those up all the time."

"Do another."

"Okay, give me a minute and let me think of one." Sam rests his tongue against his chipped tooth while he considers my request.

So incredibly cute! It makes me a teeny crazy.

He snorts. "Okay. What if Tom Petty married Johnny Cash?"

Tom Petty Cash! I crack up. This one was funnier than the first. I'm hooked and know right then I'll rack my brain trying to come up with one worthy of a snort from him.

~~~

After a couple more lunches with Sam I decide to try one. "What if Snoop Dog married Sonny Bono?

"Good one." Sam digs into his incredible pile of food. Today it's a Mexican fiesta.

I toss a packet of photos at Sam. "You asked. This is what I did over summer vacation." Pointing to pictures of John, Mom and Dad, I tell Sam a bit about each of them.

Sam looks confused. "I thought you said your summer vacation was weird. Sea World is pretty normal stuff."

"Trust me. My parents are hyper-normal, so that's not the weird thing. You asked me about my tattoo, so Sea World is part of the reason."

Yesterday when Sam asked me why a dolphin, I couldn't bring myself to tell him the story I'd told to the tattoo artist. It seemed private and…odd. But I decided to tell him about our summer vacation instead. I smile at Sam, and it feels awkward and flirty.

"At Sea World we went to the dolphin show, and I hated it. I mean, I love dolphins. I might have even been one in a past life."

"You think you're reincarnated from a dolphin? You're right. That's pretty weird."

"Maybe. John's girlfriend says so." I smile again. "But like I was saying, I hated watching them doing tricks. They looked like they were having fun, but I thought they weren't and that they'd have more fun if they were free. You know what I mean?"

Sam nods. "I've been to Sea World."

"Do you like dolphins?" I wonder aloud.

"Sure." Sam's smile is sweet.

"Why?" I know I've gotten off track on the whole Sea World story, but this is important to me.

He rubs his chin, but the smile never leaves his face. "They seem happy. Not fake happy, but genuinely happy."

He gets it.

"Exactly," I say with a hefty grin. "So, after the show we went underneath the tank to this viewing area, where we could watch them swimming around. That part was a lot cooler than the show." I pause, a little afraid to tell this next part. "Well, I just think they're beautiful. I put my hand on the viewing wall, wanting to touch them. When I did, they all swam directly at me—one after another. They'd swim right at me. Sometimes they'd come from the bottom of the tank, skimming the side and almost touching my hand."

Sam holds his tongue against his tooth, thinking.

"At first I thought, 'Maybe it just looks like they're swimming at me because the tank is round. Maybe everyone else thinks they're swimming at them too.' But they didn't. Because when I looked around to see what other people were doing, they weren't watching the dolphins. They were all staring at me."

I let out a big sigh. It's not that the story is a big deal or anything, but I haven't really talked about it with anyone other than Lexie.

"So why do you like them?" Sam asks.

I don't have a quick answer and take my time to respond. "What you said, but that's only part of it. I think it's, it's…unconditional love?" That wasn't what I expected to come out and if I'd known it ahead of time, I might have kept that to myself. It sounded kinda corny out loud.

Sam raises an eyebrow.

"Anyway," I continue, "I want to swim with them. I don't know what'll happen, but I really want to and I'm going to. I just don't know when. Wanna come?"

"Sure. You bet. I wouldn't want to miss watching Dolphin Girl."

Dolphin Girl. That's me, and Sam had figured it out.

# CHAPTER FOUR

Sam surprises me when he waits for me after English to walk to Bio.

It's the first time he's done this. Usually, he travels halfway with Ashley and then picks up Travis in the main hall. I'm normally four or five steps behind all of them.

Between classes, the pods ebb and flow. They aren't as well-defined or as large as they are before school. When Sam and I pass the bulletin board, Karen Perry says to me, "Today we're finishing all the cobwebs."

Sam gives me a funny look and I explain we're working on decorations for The Monster Mash.

"Cool. So are they gonna be good?"

"Yeah, they're good—I think—but I won't get to see how they all look together."

"Why not?"

"Grounded. No cha-cha for me." I say this jokingly, but it bums me beyond belief.

Mrs. Clavell stands in the hall, guarding the Bio lab. The bell rings as we squeeze past her, and she closes the door behind us.

Sam leans close and whispers into my ear, "You're grounded?"

My brain goes mushy from his breath against my neck.

"Mr. Rojas. Class has begun." Clavell waits for me to scurry to a lab table, and Sam ends up sitting next to me. This is new too. Usually he's on the other side of the room with Travis.

While I try to get oriented—not too easy considering my brain is on total overload—Clavell drones on and on about DNA and Francis Crick's contributions. I pretend I'm taking notes until Sam puts his hand on top of mine and then hands me a slip of paper.

*Are you kidding about not going to the dance?*

Not anymore. Every day at lunch Sam and I talk up all sorts of randomness. A part of me has been hoping he'd bring up the dance and another part thought it would just be a bitter disappointment. There's no way my mom will relent. Besides the crime has been worth the time. Totally.

*NO,* I write. *I MEAN I WAS GOING, BUT NOW I'M NOT. I'M ON AN ALCATRAZ VERSION OF HOUSE ARREST.*

I'm about to hand the note back when there's a rap on the

door. Clavell cruises between our lab tables to answer it. It's Mr. Higginbottom, the chemistry teacher from next door.

Clavell purses her lips, prim and proper. "Please read chapter two in your text," and then she follows Higginbottom out.

For exactly three seconds there's no sound. And then the room erupts.

Travis Thomlinson jumps up, puts on Clavell's lab coat and a pair of safety goggles, playing with the equipment like he's the Nutty Professor or a mad scientist or something. A lot of the kids think he's funny.

I roll my eyes. "He's a knob."

"He's all right." Sam sounds like he's apologizing.

I guess it's nice that he sticks up for his friend, but I still think Travis acts idiotic most of the time.

Connor and Emily share a chair behind their lab table and make out. They've been inseparable since freshman year and don't care who watches. I look away when Connor reaches for Emily's shirt.

"They're in love," Sam says, then snorts.

I'm not sure if it's love or some sort of DNA gender attraction thing. "Seems like." I hand him the note.

He reads it and gets a sad-puppy look on his face. "She grounded you from the dance?"

"Yeah. Like I was sayin', I won't even get to see how the

37

decorations look. It sucks."

"That's for sure." Sam repositions himself so he's facing sideways. His feet rest on the base of my stool. Our knees are almost touching.

This is different. And nice. My heart thumps a little harder. *Keep him close.* I desperately need to change the subject. If I stay all gloomy, he'll go hang with Travis. "So, what are you going as?" I act peppy.

Sam's face brightens. "I'm thinking about Elvis."

"Cool Elvis or Vegas Elvis?"

"Vegas Elvis *is* the cool Elvis," he says. "But some of the guys—Travis and Chase—are trying to get a bunch of us to go as a chain gang. They have five guys now and want me to join. It sounds cool, but we'd have to stick together the whole time."

"You couldn't even dance."

"We could. We'd just have to get partners at the same time."

I imagine those guys lined up, chained and dancing. I laugh. "I feel sorry for the guy who can't get a girl. He'll look kinda silly all by himself."

Sam leans in, his knees brushing mine. "If you were going, if you could get your mom to change her mind, would you dance with me so I'm not that guy?"

"Sure." I smile, and it's not my own. It's flirty and secretive. Mysterious. Like the Mona Lisa.

"Cool," Sam says. His foot taps my stool and ends up brushing mine. Was that on purpose? I hope so. He blushes a little and asks, "And what would you be?"

I hesitate. Because even though there's a part of me that thinks Sam likes me, there's another part that thinks if he saw my costume it would mean the end of our lunches. "You'll think it's weird."

"Tell me," he begs. "I like weird."

Hmm, maybe not this weird; maybe it's good I'm not going.

I shake my head. "It doesn't matter. My mom's not the type to change her mind."

"So you're not going to tell me?" Sam's grinning.

"No. No way." I shake my head like crazy.

My Mona Lisa smile emerges a second time because I've gotten away without telling Sam about Dolphin Girl.

~~~

An ultra-fine brush dipped in off-white paint is what I need to add cobwebs to the furniture, staircase, and chandelier. Dip. Smooth, steady stroke. Repeat. As I glance around the cafeteria, I see the other painters in deep concentration. We only have four days to finish.

Karen Perry kneels in front of another huge sheet depicting the outside of the haunted house. She's got both brass-colored and gunmetal off-black paint to give depth to the gargoyle knocker for the front door.

Adding these cobweb lines is easy, but I can tell already the color is not quite right. Too much contrast.

"What do you think I need here? Light gray?"

Karen sucks in her cheeks, making fishy lips as she studies my mural. "Try this." Her finger hovers over a few spots where I can apply light gray.

Ah! That's what it needed.

As I've gotten to know Karen, I've learned she's nothing like I thought. It's kinda like when I got paired with Nigel. At the beginning of last year, I thought he was a burnout who hung out in the courtyard all day. Mrs. Osario assigned us to be conversation buddies in Spanish. One day, after a couple of months of strange, funny dialogues about horses or butcher shops or bathrooms, and sometimes all three at once, he became just Nigel to me.

I used to think Karen was a perfectionist. Like Mom. Her clothes and hair have been ironed to the point where she could be featured in an ad for starch or something. But as it turns out, she's all right, way more relaxed than I thought. She could even fit with my water fountain friends. All this makes me wonder if she looks at me differently than she used to before we knew each other.

Karen watches me apply the light gray paint the way she

suggested. "That looks good." She pauses. "I have a question for you."

I finish the cobwebs on the chandelier and look up. "What?"

"Do you like photography? I mean, are you good at it?"

I've always been kinda interested, so I say, "Yeah. I guess so."

"Well, the reason I asked is that we need another photographer for the yearbook. We only have one. There's no way he can make it to all the activities."

Wow. That's unexpected. But just because Karen likes me doesn't mean the other yearbook kids would welcome me with open arms.

"I probably can't do it. I can't even go to the dance." I rub my hand back and forth on the mural.

"Why can't you go?"

"Grounded."

"What? Why?"

"My mom saw my tattoo and went radioactive." I wave the paint brush. "Really nuclear. It's a month long."

"A month?" Karen's mouth hangs open, like she can't believe the punishment. "That's practically a lifetime." She dips her brush into a small plastic tub of khaki-colored paint. "My mom took my sister to get a tattoo. It's a small rose."

"My mom needs to spend some time with your mom."

Karen stares at me. "Can you at least ask her? I mean, we really need another one, and yearbook is almost like a class. Maybe she'll say yes."

I don't know what's more surprising—Karen's mom getting her sister a tattoo, or her asking me to be the photographer. Seems like I should at least try. "Okay, I'll ask."

~~~

While walking home after school I end up totally engrossed in an imaginary conversation with my mom, where I'm trying to convince her to let me be a yearbook photographer. Then I hopscotch forward and in my mind, my first assignment is The Monster Mash and I'm dancing with an Elvis-styled Sam while holding a camera.

A girl can dream, can't she?

When I snap out of it, I realize I walked several blocks past my turn and then decide I should detour and go to the Chapel Lakes Preserve. It's one of my favorite spots for escaping the rules—both my mom's and the pods'—that govern my life.

The preserve sits on a piece of land ten maybe fifteen minutes from school in suburban South Florida, protected through an agreement with the Seminole Indians. It's not large, only a few walkways built above wetlands that look like the Everglades—untamed and wild. Just outside the border there are houses and strip shopping centers and gas stations, which make it a little surreal once you enter.

I walk through the empty unpaved parking lot and tiny stones crunch under my feet. Off to the side there's a trailer with a small pickup parked in front. It's the caretaker's office. I've only seen him once, and since there's never anyone else here, I can't imagine what he does all day.

The floating wooden walkway wobbles, not quite solid, as I step across and wind my way through foliage that looks so different from other places. Everything, and I do mean everything, gets professionally landscaped in South Florida's 'burbs—a cluster of palms, some low shrubs and a splash of color. It's so predictable, and you basically can't leave your house without seeing a truckload of workers making sure the surroundings stay manicured. But at this place, small plants grow wherever they bloom. Vines wind their way around trees. Some plants seed and grow off the trunks of larger trees, not even rooted to the soil. So, while it's unplanned, it's exactly as it should be.

The beauty of it takes my breath away.

I wander past signs describing colorful plants and animals found here: White Ibis, Black Mangrove and Purple Gallinule. The descriptions over time have become so ingrained that I don't need to stop and read them anymore. At the edge of the water where the walkway ends, a small roof is elevated by poles. I sit under it, cross-legged, and pull my sketch pad from my backpack.

A slight breeze swirls, a blessing during this hot, sticky time of year. Through the vegetation, I can see the busy road that runs along the edge of the preserve, but can't hear any of the car sounds, only the hum of insects and the power lines. The air shimmers at the boundary and it's like I'm sitting inside this protected bubble, separate from the world. John told me this land was important to the Seminoles. He thought it might be a burial ground.

I don't know about that, but it is something sacred.

And here's something else that's a little weird. People always say when you have water in Florida, you have two things—gators and mosquitoes. In all the times I've been here, I've never seen a gator, and I've never had a mosquito bite. I'm not saying they're not around, but they aren't in my reality.

After opening the pad to a clean sheet, I look around for something to draw. Over by a peninsula of plants that hangs into the water, an anhinga has spread his wings to dry out after fishing. I sketch his outline in the foreground and begin filling in the details surrounding him. As I work, my mind wanders.

Mom's been a lot tenser since John upset things over the summer. I probably wouldn't have a dolphin tattoo if John hadn't gotten a job at The Organic Cornucopia. Who woulda thought a tiny sandwich shop could completely change things?

At first, when John was hired, Mom and Dad were both thrilled. Most of John's friends hadn't been able to find summer jobs, and he was working long hours every day.

"Why do you get home so late?" Dad had asked one morning at breakfast.

"We do a lot of prep for the next day." John yawned, swigged the last of his juice and ran his hands through his hair. "I'm gonna go get a shower."

When he left, Mom said, "Maybe there's a girl he likes there."

Of course Mom was right. And he asked to bring her to our Fourth of July family cookout. While girls had always flocked to my brother the Trophy-Caser, he'd only brought one home before because Mom's standards were impossibly high.

On the day of the cookout, I was so curious about his date that instead of hanging out in my room with Lexie, we staked out a spot in the living room where I could watch out the big arched window. U2 played on my iPod while I doodled flags and apple pies, waiting to check out John's All-American girl. Lexie buried herself in an armchair with the most recent issue of Rolling Stone.

John's Toyota Camry pulled into the driveway and he stepped out followed by a…girl? Or was she a woman? She had wildly curly hair and was dressed in a long, tie-dyed skirt and macramé top. When she opened the back door, a creature bounded out and ran in crazy circles around her feet. I was pretty sure it was a dog but not entirely certain, because if it was, it was the strangest looking one I'd ever seen.

They say dogs often resemble their owners, but this one didn't look a bit like John's date. It had Paris Hilton's legs with Don King's hairdo.

John hadn't mentioned the dog, and I knew Mom would freak.

"They're here," I yelled toward the kitchen.

Mom wiped her hands on a dish towel and peered out the living room window. "What *is* that?"

"I think it's a dog," I replied as Lexie turned away to laugh.

John opened the front door.

His date strolled through and squeezed Mom in a huge bear hug while Mom stood, arms stiff at her sides. "Hi Liz. John's told me so much about you. I'm Desiree." Her face was free of makeup, dotted with a smattering of freckles and etched with a few lines around her bright green eyes. She was too old for John.

As soon as she broke her hold on Mom, the creature charged forward, stuck his snout in Mom's crotch and then jumped, paws on her chest. He licked her face.

Mom waved the dishrag to scare him. "No, doggie. No, no."

"That's Bob Dylan," Desiree said. "He likes you. C'mon, Dylan, that's enough lovin'. Get down." Dylan gave Mom one more big slurp and then obeyed by sitting calmly at Desiree's Birkenstock-clad feet. "I hope you don't mind that I brought him, but when John told me how late this would go, I couldn't leave him home alone with the fireworks going off."

*Oh, yeah. There will be fireworks later. Especially after you're gone.*

A ball of dog fluff floated near Mom's feet, and she compulsively reached for it with the dishtowel.

Desiree looked at me and said, "You must be Jane," then wrapped her arms around me.

I liked her even if she was too old.

After dinner, Lexie and I cleared dishes while Mom fixed dessert for everyone. She held a scoop of vanilla ice cream over a stars and stripes bowl and asked, "Where do you go to school, Desiree?" In typical Mom fashion, she'd waited until John wasn't around to ask this.

"Oh, I went to high school in Orlando and then went to college at UF, but I never really got around to finishing. I moved here about four years ago and still take classes every now and then, but when you reach twenty-nine, it's like, what's the point?"

Uh, bombshell.

Mom's knuckles grew white as the ice cream plopped onto the counter. Lexie mouthed, *twenty-nine* to me. Outside, a neighbor set off a bottle rocket.

But the fireworks I expected never materialized. At least not in front of me.

It stayed quiet until August, when John announced he'd decided not to go to UF, but rather FAU—which was only about twenty minutes from home. Because the dorms were all full, he put his name on a waiting list, scheduled his classes and kept his job at the Organic Cornucopia.

I'm pretty sure there are nights he doesn't come home. Last week, I wandered into his room a couple of days in a row, sort of wishfully thinking he'd be there or just wanting to be reminded of him. His bed was made but there was a huge bump near the middle where the sheets and blanket were bunched up. The next day, same bump, same place.

As I stood there, Mom walked in, threw back the comforter and pulled the sheets and blanket taut. "I guess he left already," she said as she smoothed the comforter into place. It made me wonder if she hadn't noticed or if she was just pretending.

~~~

The anhinga's wings finally dry and he takes flight, swirling overhead before settling onto a branch that bends and dips under his weight. The nearly completed sketch is good—tight lines but not too cramped, the way a nature sketch should be.

I glance at my watch. Only twenty minutes have elapsed. That's another amazing thing about the preserve. Time almost comes to a standstill here. I get up and stretch, arms and heart wide open like I can embrace the landscape.

When I look out over the water, I wish, as always, that a dolphin would swim up to the end of this dock. It couldn't happen, though. This spot is too far inland and not connected to the ocean. But it feels so magical here that I can't stop myself from wishing. And if it ever did, there's a part of me that wouldn't be surprised at all.

~~~

Somehow, even though I stayed after school to work on the murals and then stopped at the preserve, I still manage to finish every item on Mom's list. It's a miracle.

She walks from room to room, smiling and nodding. Finally she says, "The house looks beautiful. Thank you."

I follow her to the kitchen, where she peeks into the oven to check on the casserole. Shifting from foot to foot, I say, "I got it in on time today."

"Fantastic!" She removes the mitten potholder and places it on the counter.

"I was wondering—" I stop when Mom eyes me. "This girl in school asked if I could be a photographer for the yearbook. They only have one, and she said they need another and thought I might be good at it."

Mom rests her right elbow in her left hand, rubbing her chin.

"The thing is—I think they need a person before my grounding is over."

"Hmm. Would you be hanging out with that group of kids?"

*That Group*—my pod.

Mom was never a huge fan of Lexie, even when we were little kids. There was a time in third or fourth grade when she came over to play. We raced around the backyard, giggling and chasing John. Then we tromped, all sweaty, into the kitchen, and Lexie asked Mom for something to drink. Later on, after she'd gone home, Mom said, "That child never says 'please' or 'thank you.'"

Mom hadn't seen the look of gratitude on Lexie's face when she handed her a big glass of Gatorade, because for her it's more about what's said, but for me it's more about what's done. I can tell by looking into people's eyes if they're sad or angry. Or their smile shows if they're being sarcastic or sincere. Sometimes people say thank you, but their face is saying screw you. So, I think Mom's missing out on a huge part of communication.

Then, last April, my best friend did something Mom's never gotten over. Lexie always had this thick sheet of pale blond hair that hung to her waist, the kind everyone envies. Truly. She chopped it off into an ultra-short, spiked 'do and pierced her upper lip at the same time with a thin gold ring.

Mom freaked. At dinner, after she'd seen Lexie's new look, she ranted. "What was she thinking? It's horrible. Horrible."

"It's not a big deal, Mom."

"What is she going to do when she has to go to work? Nobody's going to hire her with that—" she twirled her finger around the edge of her lip.

I said, "When she takes it out, you can't really tell."

That's when Mom's voice took on an I'm-about-to-go-over-the edge tone. "Don't you ever think about doing that." She pointed at me and then drummed her finger on the table. "Or you, either." She stared at John.

John and I eyed each other while Mom forked up some tetrazzini. Right before she put it in her mouth, she said, "Thank God she didn't get a tattoo."

Honestly, I don't know what came over me when I smirked and said, "At least not where we can see it."

John had just taken a bite of his casserole and he barked a laugh.

"That's *not* funny," Mom said.

John covered his mouth trying to stifle the laugh, and the casserole went down the wrong way. He coughed and made these *harump* sounds. I got up, whacked him on the back, and he looked up at me with glee in his eyes.

That's when I started laughing and couldn't stop. It was this hahahaha*hiccup*hahhaha*hiccup* thing. It came from somewhere deep inside and I don't even know what struck me as funny. I kept trying to stop. I'd calm down and then it would burst out of me again.

"Stop that, Jane. What's wrong with you?" Mom tapped her finger on the table.

But I was hysterical. Really. And when I think about it now, I wonder if it was temporary insanity.

Dad, who had been silent during this whole exchange, said, "The tetrazzini came out good tonight, hon. Can I get seconds?"

At that, John cracked up too. I laughed until tears leaked from my eyes. I wrapped my arms around his shoulders and kept laughing, my head resting on his shoulder.

Mom took Dad's plate. "I don't know what's wrong with you two. I don't know what's wrong with this family." She stormed to the kitchen.

Pretty funny looking back when you consider that I'm now under house arrest for the exact thing I'd yanked her chain about. I kinda doubt she'll bend her own rules and let me be a yearbook photographer.

But she surprises me. "It sounds like a great opportunity. I've wanted you to do something during high school other than just sitting around the house. So, okay, yes."

"They might need me to take pictures at the dance," I try.

Mom eyes me with a sideways glance. "No dance. You're

grounded, in case you forgot."

Not on your life. So okay, I didn't get everything I wanted, but getting part of it—for a change—is probably the biggest shocker in a day that's been filled with the unexpected.

*Humans have always been fascinated by and drawn to dolphins. In fact, in ancient times killing a dolphin was as serious a crime as killing a man. Whether it's their intelligence, their curious friendly faces or their playful demeanor that attracts us, one thing is certain. We have been linked to them in the past and will be linked to them in the future.*
*(Excerpt:* The Magic and Mystery of Dolphins*)*

# CHAPTER FIVE

The irony of this situation is not lost on me. That song by The Pretenders about a chain gang floats through my open window for the fourth—no, fifth—time. While a song about prisoners is being played at The Monster Mash a mere three blocks from my house, I am a prisoner unable to attend. You can't even script something like that.

I'm about to close my window to block out the constant reminder of what I'm missing: the decorations, the dance. Sam. But right before it's completely shut it, I notice my screen is a little loose. Mom's been after Dad to fix it. He hasn't, and of course that begs the question about why she cuts him a lot more slack than she'd ever cut me when it comes to her To-Do list.

I wiggle the screen, and it pops off the track. My cage door is open. I could be at the school in under five minutes. Dolphin Girl hangs in my closet, but bringing her complicates escape. My stomach knots. What if I'm caught?

It seems like an hour passes while I refuse to move. I'm holding my breath. Ridiculous. I could've already been at the school. Okay. Go. With that, I'm up on my desk and out the window before I can change my mind. During the silent jog to the school, all I can think about is Sam. Will he be surprised to see me? Was he just teasing when he asked me to dance? Which costume did he go with? *Et cetera, et cetera.* Obsess, obsess.

When I reach the school cafeteria, two Bulletin-Boarders are stationed at a table outside the door. One is dressed up as Cleopatra. The other is a 60s go-go girl. Both a cash box and a spiral of red tickets sit on the table in front of them.

"Crap. I forgot my money," I say.

"Yeah. Did you forget your costume too? What are you supposed to be?" asks Cleopatra.

"I'm a teenager sneaking out of her house when she's grounded," I say in frustration, then soften my tone. "Look, can I just peek in there real quick? I'm looking for someone. I'll only be a sec."

They shrug, which I take as a yes. So I prop open the metal

doorway and hold it in place with my hip. Right away I spot Sam. Not only is he easy to pick out because of his height, but there he is linked up and shuffling around by the refreshments with all his trophy case buddies. A few people in the crowd start with a chant. I can't make out what they're saying at first and then I finally get it.

"Chain. Gang. Chain. Gang." The DJ cues up the song again. The Trophy-Casers lurch to the middle of the dance floor and Alana throws her arms around Sam.

Why'd I have to see that? It kills me. How can prison be better than freedom? I let the door close gently. "Thanks," I say to the Boarders.

"Did you find who you were looking for?" Cleopatra asks.

"Yeah." Unfortunately. "Yeah, I did."

~~~

"You're really a mess, you know?" This is the first thing Lexie says when she walks into my room. She moves a pile of clothes aside so she can sit on my bed.

Last night I texted her after I got back from my jailbreak, and she was mad I didn't call her when I was right outside the café. Then she called early this morning and wanted to stop by to commiserate. She said, "Just ask your Mom. Even those on death row get some kind of visitation."

I could hardly believe it when Mom said okay, but for no more than an hour. Amazing. She's willing to cut me some slack. Or maybe she just feels guilty about making me miss the dance.

"Wow, your closet looks great." Lexie gets up and goes over to fix a few out-of-place pieces. "What's this?" She takes out Dolphin Girl. Because Lexie's short, it drags on the floor. She looks it up and down. "Was this your costume? It is, isn't it?"

"Yep," I confess.

"Why didn't you ever show it to me? Were you unhappy about the way it turned out? Because, I mean, you shouldn't be. It's really good."

"It's weird, dontcha think?"

"It's memorable, like you." Lexie re-hangs the dolphin and hugs me. "It sucks the big one that you couldn't go last night. It was fun, but I missed you. And someone else missed you too— guess who." She bounces on my bed, pumped up by the scoop she's got.

"Who?"

"Sam Rojas."

My heart skips a beat. "Really?"

"Yeah. He asked me if you were going to be there, but I told him you were still on house arrest. I can't believe you didn't call me when you were right outside."

"I forgot my money."

"I would've paid your way!"

"I didn't have a costume."

Lexie rolls her eyes. "Speaking of costumes—you shoulda seen Sam's. It was hysterical. He got together with five other guys and they went as a chain gang. And then, the DJ kept playing that old Pretenders' song." Her voice is static, like a radio station not quite tuned in. The glimpse of Sam with my ex-bestie still stings. "And Alana hooked up with Travis. It was so gross."

Whaaa—? Travis? "You're kidding!" While this news shocks me, there's also this huge sense of relief that Alana didn't end up with Sam.

She gets up and starts putting away my clean clothes. I know Mom's never seen Lexie's neat-freak side. If she had, she'd like her better. "No. I'm not kidding." She lays a few tops in the drawer then twists her head over her shoulder. "Totally brisk tongue action with everyone watching."

"Ew. What got into her?" I ask.

"Hopefully not Travis." She smirks, and we both crack up.

But she's right because Travis makes my skin crawl, and I'm not the only girl who feels this way.

"What is it about him?' I ask.

"He's crude." She closes every dresser drawer. "And it's the way he looks at you, like he's hungry or something."

I nod in agreement and then walk over to Flipper's tank and tap on the glass. "Does it ever bother you that we're not friends with Alana anymore?" It might seem like I'm asking Flipper, but

I'm really asking Lexie.

"Not really. You know she always wanted to hang with that crowd." Lexie sits back on my bed and stretches out her legs, pointing her toes. "Don't you remember during our sleepovers, she'd go on and on about what Whitney wore or what Brittney said." She's talking about the cute identical twins who are Trophy-Casers.

"Yeah. I guess you're right. But don't you ever wonder what it would be like to hang out with them?"

She scrunches up her face. I sense I said the wrong thing and hurt her feelings. "Not if I ever, ever, ever had to kiss Travis," she says.

I laugh; she's right.

"But I can see why you're crushing on Sam. He's a cutie...and nice."

And funny. And smart. And I'm more myself around him than I am with anyone else, except maybe John. Or when I'm by myself at the preserve.

I don't say of any of this to Lexie.

"Maybe he'll come hang with us at the fountain," she says.

Right.

One of the reasons we've stayed friends for as long as we have is because she's always optimistic. But she's wrong about this. Because the odds of Sam ending up in the water fountain crowd are about the same as me ending up in the trophy case:

slim to none.

~~~

Sam sets his pizza-laden tray across from me and says, "If J Lo married Rob Lowe—"

I laugh. "She'd be J Lo Lowe."

He tosses a packet of pictures on my lunch tray. This whole scene is like déjà vu of the day I brought Sam my summer vacation pictures. The lame name game. Sharing pictures. Except this time Sam brought the photos for me.

"What's this?" I ask.

"They're from the Mash."

"Cool," I say. But it's not really. Why torture myself about not being there? At the same time, I don't want to be rude.

I flip through them slowly, careful not to leave fingerprints. There are a couple pictures of the chain gang—Sam, Travis, Chase, Alex, Brian and some other kid I don't know. When I say, "It's the whole trophy case crowd," Sam shrugs.

Next, there's a close-up of Travis making out with Alana.

"God, Sam! We're you right in their faces?"

"He was next to me in the chain. Like, this close." Sam puts his face so close to mine. His lips are right there—mere inches from mine. *Kiss me*, I say mentally. Then he pulls back. "I couldn't get away, so I decided to capture the romance on film."

This cracks me up, and I go back to the pictures. The next few are boring. And then one really gets my blood pumping. Sam's got Alana tucked under his arm. She's dressed in a black cat costume, her arms wrapped around Sam's waist hugging him from the side. The picture reminds me of when my three-year-old cousin grabs me by the leg and I can't shake him off. It's almost exactly what I spied from the door. In fact, it might be.

I want to claw the picture. "Never cross the path of a black cat. It's bad luck."

Sam snorts. "Hey, I know how to handle cats."

What exactly does that mean?

I flip through a few more pictures—one of Ashley and Chase looking like models straight from a magazine. All of a sudden, I'm looking at a picture of the mural I painted of the foyer of a haunted house. The style, *tromp l'oeil*, is supposed to give the illusion of 3-D and I nailed it. The foyer looks great, spooky in the dim lighting. I'd only seen them in the harsh florescent lighting of the art room and cafeteria.

Next is the dining room mural. The photo is so clear you can see the cobwebs I painted on the chandelier. I keep flipping on and on. Sam took a picture of every single mural, even the ones done by other kids.

I hold my breath—a dolphin that hasn't surfaced for a while and needs fresh air. Barely audible, I fumble, "What? Why?"

"Well, you talked about these decorations non-stop. I

thought you'd want to see them hanging, but I gotta tell you, the other members thought I was crazy."

"Huh?"

"The chain gang. I dragged them around while I took pictures."

"You..." I start. "They...I mean, everybody was with you?"

"Yep."

I can't believe he did that for me. I can't believe he made all the other Casers do it too. In shock, I barely manage a thanks.

Sam raises his eyebrows, tongue resting on his tooth. "You broke your promise. You didn't dance with me," he teases.

I almost tell Sam about sneaking out, but instead I blurt, "You wouldn't have wanted to dance with me once you saw my costume."

"What were you coming as? You can tell me now. There's no reason to keep it a big secret."

"Well," I act bashful. "It wasn't a cute little kitty cat." I'm still annoyed about the pictures with Alana.

"I never thought you'd be something so common," he says.

I hesitate because I don't know how Sam will react, then bat my eyes. "I was going to be Dolphin Girl. She has a pink bow, pearl necklace and pretty lashes. She's quite feminine, actually."

Sam snorts and cracks up. As his face turns bright red, he lays his head on the cafeteria table, catches his breath and mouths the words, "You kill me."

# CHAPTER SIX

Before the first bell, I lean against the wall with my backpack bumping into the water fountain. Lexie's running band names by me for approval, but I'm only partly listening, because the rest of my attention is on Sam as he talks to Travis and Alex.

"Garage Girls?" she asks.

I wobble my hand back and forth. "Maybe."

"I'm still undecided about Estrogen Ocean."

That one is not my fave, but the art is ready to go. I bobble my head because I'm so not into this. I love Lexie, but Sam's more interesting right now.

He just told a joke or heard a joke. I can tell, because he snorts, laughs, and his face turns bright red. Alana stands with Whitney, Brittney and Ashley next to Sam. It looks like she bumps him intentionally. Sam and the boys absorb the popular girls like sponges. One big circle of cool kids.

When Sam glances in my direction, I face Lexie, pretending to be involved in her band-name dilemma. I don't want him to think I'm gaga over him or a stalker-chick.

"Are you listening?" Lexie asks me.

"Uh-huh," I lie.

The next thing I know Sam's leaning into Alana, nodding while she talks. She grabs his forearm and shakes it to emphasize her story, and the whole group cracks up.

When I face Lexie, she's watching me watch Sam laugh at a girl who used to be our friend. "You can't let it bother you." She shakes her head.

Good old Lexie. She knows I've got it bad for Sam, but I'm not sure if she means him or Alana this time. I think I heard pity in her voice.

Mercifully, the bell rings.

~~~

Between second and third periods, I stop at the bathroom in the Fine Arts hall. It's my favorite because it's never crowded. Except today, it is. There's a group of girls huddled in front of the mirrors re-applying make-up and styling their hair. At the far sink, Ashley gossips with Alana.

When Alana sees me her lip curls into something that's not a smile and she intentionally turns her back to me. Clearly I'm not invited to talk. I'm barely allowed to exist.

Unfortunately, the only open stall is the one directly behind their sink. I go in and lock the door. As I unzip my pants, I overhear Alana tell Ashley what she and Travis did over the weekend. Ew. She didn't lose her mind the night of the dance. It's been missing in action for two weeks.

Afterwards, I step up to the sink next to theirs to wash my hands.

"So then, is he a boyfriend in training?" Ashley asks.

"More like a friend with benefits." Alana dabs on some lip gloss. "I have my eye on someone else."

As I soap my hands and eavesdrop, I think, *She's so different from the girl I knew in middle school.*

"Who?" Ashley asks.

When Alana replies "Sam Rojas," I freeze and watch the water wash soap bubbles down the drain.

They must realize I'm eavesdropping because Alana notices I've turned to stone and asks me, "Are you okay?"

I grab a brown paper towel and dry my hands. "Yeah. I just zoned out for a minute."

Alana laughs and turns back to Ashley. "Where was I? Oh yeah, Sam. Travis is his best friend, so that's a little weird and all, but he's so hot."

Re-shouldering my backpack, I turn and head for the door while Ashley nods in my direction. "He is, but you'll have to get in line."

Oh God. Does that mean Ashley likes him too? Or that she knows how I feel?

~~~

I snag a tuna sandwich and lemonade as I work my way through the lunch line. Two freshmen girls giggle in front of me. They make me sentimental for a girly, gossipy lunch, like the ones I had last year with Lexie.

The line comes to a halt as we reach the cashier, and I overhear a snippet from the girl farthest from me. "He's so cute. I'm pretty sure he's a junior."

Are they talking about Sam?

"He must be madly in love with that tall girl. They eat lunch together every day," the girl closest to me says.

Are they talking about *me*?

The girl farthest from me glances in my direction and catches my eye. I smile openly at her because I don't want to make her feel bad or let on that I overheard them. She gives her friend a nudge and cranes her neck in my direction before obviously changing the subject to a new shoe store.

How strange to have someone gossiping about me and Sam. It's sweet—and a teeny bit awesome—that they think he's madly in love with me. I can't even figure out if he's madly in *like*, though.

As I put my tray down across from him, he asks, "Have you started your paper for Breckenridge?" I gaze at Sam while he waits for me to answer. Lately, he's really been bugging me about this assignment.

Actually, there are two reasons I'm annoyed with him. One—he's nagging me, but also, two—he's too attractive to others—namely Alana and Ashley, but also those freshmen girls. And who knows how many more. I don't stand a chance.

I swallow hard. "Are you my mother?"

"No, I'm your friend."

The words hang there.

Friends eat lunch together every day and occasionally walk from English to Biology. They don't say hi in the morning or speak in the hallways. They barely acknowledge each other in English, but pass notes and talk in Biology. Conversations during the weekends are off-limits, but conversations about weekends are not.

The rules of the game we're playing really suck.

"You okay?" Sam asks.

"I'm fine," I say.

"You sure?"

"Hey if Tweety Bird marries Conway Twitty—" I've been saving this one.

Sam laughs hard and rests his hand on mine. My stomach

trembles. What was it that was bugging me again?

Later on, Sam waits outside English to walk me to Bio for the second day in a row, but who's counting? We turn the corner into the main hall and practically run into Alana right in front of the trophy case.

"Hey, you." She rests her hand on Sam's chest, ignoring me. "A bunch of us wanna play Rock Band tonight. Are you up for that?"

Sam looks at me, and I'm not sure what this means. He thinks I should be asked too? He doesn't want to answer in front of me?

"You can come too, Jane," Alana says. I can hear the phony.

I shake my head no and try to sound lighthearted. "I think I have a date with a thirty-five millimeter camera tonight. I need to get to know its parts, intimately."

Sam laughs. He knows I'm still grounded, and Alana knows I got the position as the second photographer because she's one of the editors. Working on yearbook together might help us mend our friendship.

"Next time then?" She doesn't mean this either. I guess this is as chummy as it gets these days.

"Yeah, maybe." Just play along. "Hey, I just remembered I have to stop by the media center. See you guys later." I make an about-face and take off down the Language Arts hall.

I don't fit in with them. Understatement! But with how I feel about Sam and the new yearbook thing, I'm not sure where I belong.

~~~

Clavell lectures us about the reproductive systems of plants. Sam passes me a note and waggles his eyebrows. It reads:

*Pistels + Stamens = Stimulating!*

I clap a hand over my mouth, but part of my laugh burbles out anyway. Clavell glares a warning at me.

Should I have laughed? His note was funny, but is that what Alana or one of her friends would have done? Does it make me look trashy?

Sam makes invisible loop-de-loops in the air and points at me, but I fold the note and stick it in my backpack. He pouts when I don't play along.

I rip a sheet of paper from my notebook and smile at Sam. Flirt, flirt. But before I can fire off a reply, Clavell says, "Pick a partner," and she weaves around the room, placing study guides on each lab table. I face Sam, assuming we'll be partners, but Travis flies across the room.

He taps the shoulder of the kid who sits in front of Sam. "Hey, why don't you move?" He thumbs in the direction of his table on the other side of the room.

I wait for Sam to tell Travis he's going to study with me, but instead he asks Travis the first question from the guide.

Meanwhile, Brendon/Brandon, who sits in front of me, turns around. "Here, quiz me first, Jane."

For the remainder of class, we study for tomorrow's test, but I don't concentrate because I'm paying more attention to Sam and Travis's conversation than I am to Brendon/Brandon's questions. This is a mistake, a huge mistake. This kid knows science. When the dismissal bell rings, Sam says, "Later, Janey," as he strolls from the room with Travis.

Later. Great. But which Sam will I get?

I head directly to the Journalism lab, HQ for both the newspaper and yearbook. Karen Perry is in waiting there for me with a heavyset kid who's wearing thick glasses. "Jane, this is Irwin, the other photographer. Irwin, Jane."

"You can call me Tad. Everyone does." He looks at the floor and pushes his glasses up when he says this.

Karen shakes her head and mouths, "No, we don't."

I've never seen this kid before. His black hair and clothes are unruly, like he went to bed, got up and came straight to school. There's a bright red spot of acne on his chin. I wonder what pod he's in.

He scowls at me. "Did you bring the camera?"

I reach into my backpack and pull out the Nikon I checked out earlier in the day. I hold it out like I'm offering him a gift.

"Good. Now, you know what you're doing, right?"

I don't. All the pictures I've taken at home were on my dad's digital. "No, I've never used a thirty-five millimeter before. Can't I just use my digital?"

Irwin shakes his head and says to Karen like I'm not there, "Couldn't you find me an assistant who knows what to do? She's clueless. Now I have to take pictures *and* train her." He shuffles off, head down, to a bookcase and pulls three books off the shelf. Then he shuffles back and hands them to me, never looking up from the floor. "No. You can*not* use your digital. With this camera and film you'll get sixteen million pixels, give or take. Can your digital do that?"

I'm not entirely sure what a pixel is, so I stay mum.

"Read these. I can't even talk to you before then."

I take the books and juggle them with the camera but finally manage to get everything packed away. "Okay, thanks. If I need to look for you in the morning before classes, where do you hang out?"

For the first time, Irwin looks me in the face. The lenses of his glasses are smudged so badly I don't know how he can see out of them. His tone is biting. "The darkroom. That's where you'll find me."

# CHAPTER SEVEN

I should be working through mom's list or reading one of the three tomes Irwin gave me, but it's Friday afternoon and I have the whole weekend under house arrest to do those things. So at my desk, I sketch a daisy that could be the second object for my 11th grade mobile. I write parts of my day with Sam on each petal: lunch, morning hall, biology. As I draw, I'm thinking, *He loves me, he loves me not.*

I toss the flower aside because I don't know if daisies have an odd or an even number of petals.

Distracted, I switch on my laptop, launch the Internet and select the Dolphins Plus bookmark to visit the site for the bazillionth time. Dolphins Plus is an attraction in Key Largo where you can swim with the dolphins. They offer two options—you can go for a hands-on educational experience or swim with them unsupervised, no touching allowed. I want to do both. Fortunately they have a combo package.

About a month ago, I printed the information and price list. "This is all I want for Christmas," I told Mom and Dad, handing them the pages.

Mom raised her eyebrows at Dad. "Looks dangerous. We'll see."

I'm about to print a page to hang on the fridge as a reminder when I hear my bedroom door open. I twist, expecting Mom, but see John instead.

"Janey-bo-baney!" He smiles wide, walks over and kisses me on top of my head.

"I was starting to think I'd never see you again." I click on the print button.

John sprawls on my bed, one arm tucked beneath his head, staring at the ceiling. "What's the casserole du jour?"

"No casserole. Mom's making Pink Pasta, Caesar salad—"

"And garlic bread." John finishes the sentence for me because Mom, if anything, is predictable. "I picked the right night for dinner."

Pink Pasta is what John and I call Mom's Penne Rosa, which is really Penne alla Vodka on the wagon. It's a favorite for both of us.

After picking up my sketch pad and soft black pencil, I lean into the back of my desk chair. "How's Desiree?" I make an outline of a head and scrutinize John's face. He's got a scruffy beard, and his side burns are longer than the last time I saw him.

"She's—" John pauses.

I stop sketching. "She's what?"

John scratches his head and then pushes the hair away from his eyes. "Good. She's good." He gets up from the bed and roams around my room, touching the mobiles. "Remember this?" He's touching a snapshot of himself on my sixth grade mobile.

The photo shows John on his skateboard in our driveway. He'd popped it up and gripped the nose while I rotated the camera to a forty-five degree angle. In the printed black and white photo, John is vertical with a huge grin, but the background looks like we live on a steep incline. There are no hills in South Florida, but I'd made it look that way. The world— my world—was completely out of whack, but John wasn't. I loved this photo.

When I showed it to Mom she said, "Great expression on John, but it's crooked."

She didn't get it. I wonder what Irwin would think of it.

"I'm going to be a photographer for the yearbook." I pat the camera on my desk.

"Cool." John walks over to the fish bowl. "Hey Flipper, how you doin' boy?"

"He's good," I say, not looking up. "Give him a little food, would ya?"

John sprinkles food in the bowl, telling Flipper to keep swimming, buddy. Then he wanders to my closet and inspects Dolphin Girl. "I like it. You would have really stood out."

"So you heard? I'm under house arrest 'til November twenty-third."

"Yeah. Bummer. Mom told me all about it."

I thunk my forehead on the desk. I can just imagine the tone of the conversation, where Mom is concerned about me and seeking John's advice because he's the only one who understands me. Blah, blah, blah. "When did she tell you? What did she say?"

"I stopped here one morning after you left for school, but Mom hadn't left for work yet, so I got a lecture about the example I was setting for you. She blamed me for your tattoo." John pulls my costume out of the closet and holds it while imitating Mom's tone perfectly. "You know Jane's peculiar to begin with. She doesn't need any more encouragement."

"She called me peculiar? What did you say?"

"I said you're a good kid and that she should give you some space."

Dolphin Girl's head bobs, so it looks like she's agreeing with him.

Wow! I can't believe he said that to Mom. "Thanks." I beam at him when he re-hangs the costume.

I stare at John and then look back down at the sketch. The

facial features on the paper aren't his. Deep set, dark eyes look at me over high cheekbones. I fill in the last details: straight nose, full lips, slightly chipped front tooth. Sam's face stares at me and I think it's pretty good, considering I don't have a picture or the living, breathing person in front of me. I toss the sketch to the side and start another.

John stands over me and picks up the sketch. "Hey! That's not me."

"Cool your jets. I'll do you now."

"Who is this?"

"Just this guy I eat lunch with every day. Don't be so nosy." I take the sketch from John and pin it in to my coral reef bulletin board.

"So you like him." It's not even a question.

"Yeah."

"And he likes you."

"I'm not too sure about that." I rip a clean sheet from the sketchbook and smooth it out.

"He eats lunch with you. I don't think he hates you."

"I suppose."

John's leans over my shoulder to watch me work. "Have you gone out with him yet?"

I look up and give John a have-you-lost-your-mind? look. *"House arrest!"*

"Oh, yeah." John studies Sam's face on the corkboard. "He

looks like a nice guy." He points to another sketch of Sam pinned next to the one I just finished. It's a full-body sketch, fully clothed of course. "That's him too, right?"

"Yeah." My pencil makes the basic shape of John's face at an angle.

He slumps on to my bed. "So when am I going to meet him?"

"Not gonna happen." I jot light hash marks where I want to place John's features, then sketch the outline of where his scruffy beard will go. "He hangs by the trophy case, and you know I'm strictly a water fountain kind of gal."

"Nobody cares about that stuff once you're out of high school."

Giving him a yeah-right glance, I say, "Mom cares."

John flops sideways and stares at me. "Mom's in a group all her own."

I laugh. "Don't move so much. You make it hard to draw you. You're right," I say, referring to Mom. "But, I don't know. I wish he and I were in the same group. It'd make everything a lot easier." Now I'm adding highlights to his hair.

"So, you want me to teach you how to hang with the trophy case?" he asks.

I don't—not really. I don't like Whitney or Ashley or Travis. I used to like Alana, but can't tell yet if we'll ever be friends again. But the problem is, I like Sam a lot. "Could you?" I add John's mouth and nose to the sketch.

John frowns when I say that. "I have another idea." He pushes my sketch stuff aside to get my full attention and puts his palms together. "You have to see him away from school. Not with a ton of other kids around, but alone. That way you'll figure out what's what."

"No one else eats lunch with us."

"Doesn't count. It's still at school, so there's still school stuff going on." John is suggesting the impossible. "So, what are you gonna do?" he asks. He grabs last year's yearbook off my shelf and flips through the pages. Like he's bored with this conversation or he's already done his part.

"You're nuts," I say.

"Why don't you ask him over after school to listen to music?"

I think John has lost his mind. It's a lame idea that would never work. "He wouldn't come."

"He might. You have to think about how you ask." His words become mumbles to me because as he's explaining how to ask I'm struck by an idea that might work.

"I could take him to the preserve," I interrupt. "I could tell him that's where I most feel like Dolphin Girl. I think he might be curious." John raises an eyebrow. "It's a nickname he gave me," I explain.

John bobbles his head back and forth as he mulls it over.

"That might work. You sure he's okay, not a dawg or anything?"

It's sweet John's worried about me, but I'm not. "He's fine."

He folds the yearbook closed. "Let me see." John grabs my sketch of him and inspects it. "How do you do that?"

"It's no big deal." I tuck the pencil behind my ear. "You have to look at each piece as separate, just focus on one little thing at a time and pay close attention. Most people don't want to pay close attention. Or they get overwhelmed by the whole thing in front of them instead of working through one detail. Really, anyone can do it."

I can tell he doesn't believe me. I'm not even sure *I* believe me. It sounds too much like Mom's approach to housekeeping and life. That's frightening, because we're not at all alike and I refuse to end up that way. I look at Dolphin Girl in the closet, but her head isn't bobbing. I can't even tell if she believes me.

John hangs with me for the rest of the afternoon, and we talk about all sorts of randomness exactly the way we used to before college and Desiree. When Mom calls both of us to dinner I remember what I was doing when he dropped in.

"Go talk to her for a minute. I need to look something up." When John leaves, I Google daisies + number of petals. The first site talks all about the math of daisies—Fibonacci numbers and sequences in nature. Interesting, but I don't have time to read, so I bookmark this page for later.

Where's the petal information? Oh, daisies come in 34, 55 and 89 petal varieties. Who knew? I use my limited math skills to calculate I have a two out of three chance Sam loves me. Not too shabby. Armed with this newfound wisdom, I'm ready to face another family meal.

Everyone has dished up their plates by the time I reach the table. Mom hands me a large ceramic bowl of Pink Pasta before I take my seat. "How was yearbook? Is the other photographer nice?"

Irwin is not what Mom had in mind when she wanted me to broaden my group of friends.

"Great." I scoop some pasta onto my plate. "His name is Irwin."

Mom's brows furrow when I say this.

"But everyone calls him Tad. He gave me three photography books to read." I take the salad bowl from John. His expression is wary.

"That's nice," Mom says and turns to John, "Do you know Tad?"

"Yes. I know…Tad. He takes all the sports shots." I'm grateful John plays along with me. Because if he knows Irwin, he also knows I'm withholding information Mom would deem critical.

We eat in silence for a few minutes then Mom asks, "Where's Desiree tonight? I hope you two haven't had a fight or anything?" She uses what John calls her plastic flowers voice.

John dishes himself more pasta. "She's at work."

"She works too hard. She should have asked for the night off." Still fake.

"She's been putting in extra time." John swipes his garlic bread through leftover dressing in his empty salad bowl. "'Cause in four months she'll need time off for the baby."

*What?* Did he say baby? I must have been daydreaming about Sam or something because there's no way he said that. I lean forward, elbows on table.

John's palms are flat on the table. "We're having a baby."

WTF! He did.

Mom takes a bite of her food and says in this matter of fact tone, "You can't have a baby. You're too young to have a child." It's so weird that she's acting all calm like that. God, look how she freaked over my tattoo.

"It's a little late for that," John says.

I flop against the chair, stunned. I can't believe we spent all afternoon together, and he didn't tell me.

Mom props her elbow on the table and rubs her forehead. "I'm sure it's not too late. How far along is she?"

"What does that mean?" John's voice booms.

Mom arches one eyebrow. "What about everything you've worked for?" Her finger is poised for a tap, and Dad puts his hand over hers. "You need to think about your future." This is definitely not a part of her plans for John.

"This *is* my future."

"Be responsible, John," Mom manages. "You're not making sense."

"Responsible is exactly what I am being."

I'm still stuck on the word *baby*, but force myself to focus on the conversation.

Dad puts an arm on John's shoulder. "You sprung this on us a bit. Let's see if we can't all calm down and discuss this reasonably."

Mom's mouth tightens as she pushes away from the table and stares at the ceiling, searching for an answer. Her head rolls down and she stares at John. "John, you have no idea. Babies— not just babies, children—are a huge responsibility. It's a life besides your own that—" She stops. "It's an obligation like no other. So many things can go wrong."

John swallows hard.

"Right, hon?" Mom's asking Dad for support.

Dad strokes Mom's hand and says, "You're right." He looks to John. "I do like that girl a lot." Technically speaking, Desiree's not a girl; she falls somewhere in between John and my parents. But Dad's mellow comment cools the conversation. "I guess we should say congratulations."

Mom starts to tap out 'SOS' in Morse code, but Dad's hand stifles her again. She closes her eyes and her shoulders slump.

"Have you decided when the wedding will be?"

Perfect. Of course, appearances matter to her.

"We were married yesterday. Desiree didn't want anything big. That's why I came by tonight—to tell you."

Mom gasps and pulls her hand from under Dad's. She snatches everyone's plates and scrapes the remains into the serving bowl.

I wasn't done eating. I hadn't even started.

"Jane, help me with dishes. In the kitchen."

I clear a few things. Mom's already standing over the dishwasher, bowls and silverware clattering. Working back and forth between the table and kitchen is like travelling between two foreign countries. Dad and John huddle with hushed voices; Mom makes as much noise as possible.

I don't belong with either one and that's okay, I guess. It's not my crisis this time. In fact, I'm not sure it's a crisis at all. Sure, for Mom it is, but John's always been an excellent big brother and I'm sure he'll make an excellent father, too. I just don't understand why he didn't use a condom. I mean c'mon, eighth grade Sex Ed. Duh.

As I clear the last of the food, Dad stands by the front door with John and gives him a bear hug. In the kitchen, Mom uses the counter as a crutch. She's crying as she hangs onto it. Dad approaches her from behind and wraps his arms around her, but she throws his arms off and glares at him. She's silent-treatment angry.

"Liz, I'll be upstairs when you want to talk," Dad says.

As I wipe the counters down with the sponge, Mom flings open the junk drawer. She piles thread, chewing gum, batteries, picture hangers, matches, shoelaces and a bunch of stuff I can't identify onto the counter and wordlessly begins to sort it back into the compartments in the drawer organizer.

Does she really think that will make everything better?

# CHAPTER EIGHT

Shutter speeds? Condenser lens? I can't concentrate on the book Irwin gave me because my mind keeps replaying our catastrophic family dinner.

There's a steady *thwock thwock* on my bedroom window. Lifting the blinds, I see Lexie's grinning face outside.

I flip the latch and open the window. "Hey, what are you doing?"

Willow and Tara lurk on the sidewalk over by Lexie's mom's Jeep.

"We decided to go pool hopping. It wouldn't be the same without you, sooo…you have to come."

"I'm grounded, remember?"

"Duh. That's why I'm knocking on your window instead of the front door. C'mon, sneak out."

I tip my head in the direction of the street. "How'd you

convince your mom to let you have the Jeep?" Lexie usually drives her brother's hand-me-down car.

"I didn't, so I'm breaking rules, too. C'mon, are you in?"

It sounds fun. Like something we'd do on a hunt. Willow is jumping like she's on a pogo stick, and Tara waves like a maniac. I shake my head. "Okay, okay. Give me a few minutes to make sure the coast is clear."

I tiptoe out of my room and glance upstairs. There's no light underneath my parents' bedroom door, but I can hear the muffled sounds of their TV. I wonder if they've talked yet, or if they're watching a program, or if they've both conked out and left the TV on. I decide to risk it and head back into my bedroom, slipping out the window quietly.

The Jeep's parked two houses down. Trying not to make any noise, I run diagonally through a couple front yards and hop in the front seat. Willow squeezes my shoulder and when I turn around, she and Tara do our crank-it-up dance.

"We're headed to Willow's neighborhood. Fewer screens, y'know?" Lexie puts the car in first and pulls away.

Willow's neighborhood is where I wish we lived. Even though it's older, the houses all sit on yards that are ginormous by Florida standards. Because of this, a lot of the homes don't put screens around their patios or pools, leaving everything more open. This makes it a lot easier to hop. If dolphins had to live out of the water, this neighborhood is where they'd choose to live.

It's a little cool out tonight and I shiver, glad I threw on a Roxy sweatshirt. I start to twirl my hair into an elastic, then decide to let it blow all over the place. Lexie's punky pale blond hair whips around like confetti in the moonlight.

Our wheels show how far apart her Mom is from mine. My Mom drives a Lexus. I love the Jeep's bumpy, adventurous, open-to-the-elements drive.

When we turn onto Ixora Way, Willow says, "Don't park on my street. Go down to that cul-de-sac."

Lexie edges the Jeep against a curb and we leave our shoes in the car, sneaking barefoot into the backyard of a huge rambling one-story with a circular driveway covered by a roof that extends from the house to keep the owners dry during rainstorms. Nice. There isn't a car parked in it or anywhere else we can see. With all the lights out, it's a safe place to start.

Fresh cut grass tickles my bare feet as a dog starts barking a couple houses over. It sounds as big as a Clydesdale, so I hope he's fenced. We all take turns jumping in one end of the pool, swimming the length and crawling out the other end. What a rush!

That water's warm. The pool must be heated. A soft nighttime breeze swirls around us as we giggle, trying to be silent as we jog through a yard without a pool. Another dog, a small, yippy one, joins the other in barking, but it doesn't discourage us.

In and out at the next pool. One after another.

It's awesome.

My sweatshirt and jean shorts droop as water drips down my legs.

When we reach the edge of the next yard, Lexie says, "I'm going *au natural*." Her grin, and the way she wiggles her eyebrows is a dare. She shimmies out of her clothes and the next thing I see is her pale butt running toward the pool.

Willow's halfway undressed and Tara, who never needs a prod, has already taken off. Naked.

I strip and motion for Willow to go first. After she's in and out of the pool, I sprint, wind against my skin, and then dive. When I glide underwater, something inside of me cascades into place. Silence. Calm. The way the water feels without a suit—silky—returns me to dolphin life. As I pull myself out of the pool, the others are heading back to get dressed, but I take off for the next one.

My drenched hair slaps against my back as I fly through the next pool-less yard. Glancing over my shoulder, I realize my nudist friends are laughing and running after me, clothes held in front of them. But I won't stop, can't stop.

I'm free. I'm free.

Ahead, there's an enormous pool. It's not exactly Olympic-sized but it's huge and rectangular, made for swimming laps. I don't slow a bit as I come to the edge but adjust to a flatter dive since the pool's not very deep. I swim under water and surface at the center, the water barely covering my chest when standing.

Oh, God! There's a group from the trophy case in that house. On the other side of sliding glass doors, in a brightly lit den, they're playing Rock Band.

*Please don't see me. Please, please, please.*

Ashley Grant gets up off the couch and walks toward the doors. I duck underwater. Why can't I just disappear? Bubbles escape my nose and mouth. Maybe I could just drown? That way, even if I'm found naked, I won't have to be embarrassed because I'll be dead.

I blow out the last of my air and let my head surface like a periscope. Now Ashley is holding the mic, Chase Dunne is on drums and Alana on guitar. Travis sits on the couch behind all of them and grabs Alana around the waist, pulling her into his lap. *Get me out of here!* She laughs and gives Travis a quick hug.

In middle school, during our sleepovers, Lexie, Alana and I talked all night about the mystery of boys—about what they wanted and the girls who attracted them. We never figured it out then, but it looks like Alana finally did.

I, on the other hand, am a naked submarine, spying just beyond enemy lines. Without a clue about boys or Trophy-Casers or popularity. None of these people are my friends. Then, it hits me. Where's Sam? This is, after all, his pod.

As my eyes gradually adjust to the lighting, I notice a

shadow on one of the lawn chairs. It snorts—a laugh I know all too well. The tall, gangly outline stands, takes a step closer to the pool. "Jane, is that you?"

Omigod! OMIGOD! The sub siren sounds ah-OOG-ah, ah-OOG-ah. Dive, dive, dive. I submerge again, knowing this does nothing—not even cooling off the heat that has spread over every inch of my body and face. I'm so hot from embarrassment, I expect the pool to begin boiling any minute now.

I want to drown, but my body won't let me. I gasp as I surface.

"It is you," he says.

"It's me," I confess. I can hear my friends giggling. They sound oceans away.

Sam grins at me. "This is an interesting situation."

"Sam!" I use my hands to conceal as much as I can. It'd be better to be an octopus right now. "Please don't tell them I'm out here. Please." I nod toward the doors.

"I won't."

I look over my shoulder and see Lexie, Willow and Tara at the edge of the yard. I'm pretty sure Sam hasn't noticed them when Lexie steps beside him. "Do you have a towel?"

"Aw, man. You are such a buzzkill," Sam says to Lexie as he saunters to a patio chair and grabs a bright red beach towel. He walks back to the pool and holds it, his arms open wide.

He's kidding, right? I can't get out like this.

Lexie giggles. She's lost her mind.

"I'll close my eyes," he says. "I promise."

"Get real, Rojas. Lexie jerks the towel from his hands, and Sam laughs.

"A guy's gotta at least try."

Lexie holds the towel open, a shield between Sam and me. The best thing is, I'm as red as the towel, so maybe it'll act like camo. I hoist myself from the pool. Water drizzles off me. I wrap the towel around and tuck the corner under the top edge. A huge sigh of relief escapes now that I'm semi-decent.

"I think you owe me one," Sam says.

Yikes! And what will payback be? I pull the towel tighter.

Sam tips his head toward the sliding doors. "I better get back inside before somebody comes looking for me."

"Yeah." I smile shyly.

After the door closes, Lexie hands me my sopping jean shorts and sweatshirt so I can get dressed on the side of the house. Behind some hedges, I shiver while slipping into them. Cold? Fear? Both. My gaze drifts to the backyard and through the patio door, I can see Sam playing lead singer, toy mic in hand.

A few minutes ago there was very little separating Sam from me. A little terry cloth, that's all. The glass of the patio door feels more secure.

Yep. Definitely much safer.

~~~

On Monday, I take a deep breath before stepping into the cafeteria, because I haven't talked to Sam since Friday night. As if high school wasn't quite awkward enough for me. Doesn't everyone hide a little bit of themselves?

Except me.

On Friday night.

When I was buck naked.

After paying the cashier, I wonder if I could sit at another table, but Sam's already at our regular one, waving me over. I smile but don't meet his eyes as I sit across from him.

"Nice to *see* you," Sam says.

Honestly, I can't look up from my tuna sandwich and meet his eyes.

He snorts a laugh. "Why were you in my pool this weekend?"

Oh God! I didn't realize it was *his* house. Why didn't Willow stop me?

"We were just messing around. Pool-hopping. I didn't know it was your place. We never see each other outside of school, y'know?" I take a quick bite of the sandwich so I'll shut up.

"I saw a lot of you this weekend." Sam snorts a laugh. "Correction. I saw all of you."

The heat in my face must be turning me raspberry red. I'm in full-blush mode when Alana and Karen Perry stroll up. What are they doing here? It's not their lunch hour.

"Hey, Sam!" Alana says. "Ready for the big meet today?"

I'd forgotten all about that—the Regionals today—because I'd been so worried about the whole naked thing.

Karen Perry says, "Good luck," then turns to me. "We were looking for you. Can you go to the meet? We need pics, and Irwin can't go."

A chance to see Sam swim? I nod at Karen. "Yeah."

She hands me one document after another. "Okay. Here's your press pass. That will let you in for free. And here's the pass for early release from your last class."

Sam and I will leave Biology together. Can this day get any better?

"We got you a spot in the swim van. You need to be out front at two-thirty," Karen says. "Don't forget to stop by the darkroom to check out a camera."

Sam grins at me. "I guess it's only fair. I saw you in the pool, and now you'll see me. Except I'll be dressed." He snorts again.

And I feel the raspberry return.

~~~

**Shel Delisle**

At 2:30, the group going to Regionals waits in the loop for the van to arrive. There are thirteen of us. The ten swimmers—six girls and four boys—are juniors and seniors. The team manager, the assistant coach, and I are the other passengers.

I can't believe my lousy luck when Alana walks up. "You didn't tell me you were coming," I say.

"I have to write the copy for this spread." She says it like this is the last place she'd want to be. "And then Mr. Fischer asked me if I could cover it for the school newspaper. I needed another assignment like I needed a hole in the head."

Yeah. Right. I wonder how she finagled this.

Both of us want to be here because of Sam, but he stands separate from everyone with his iPod plugged into his ears. His posture is erect and his eyes are trained on some point in the distance.

When Mr. Leonard, the swim coach, swings the van into the loop, the swimmers step back, letting the rest of us go first. I follow Alana through the side door but sit in the row behind her, next to the team manager and assistant coach. Then the swimmers file on board. A group of the girls sit in Alana's row. When Sam eases into the seat next to me, he gives me one quick smile and then looks straight ahead, sprawling his legs into the gap between the seat and the sliding door.

*Ha. I get to sit next to Sam.* I know that petty voice is jealousy. Not cool, but I can't help the way I feel.

94

Alana turns halfway around in her seat, reaches her arm over the back and taps him on the knee. Sam pulls out the ear bud. "I need to ask you a few questions for the article I'm writing," she says.

"After the meet." Sam sticks the bud back in. Discussion over.

No way am I going to try to strike up a conversation, so I keep myself busy by fiddling with the camera.

After a bit, Sam glances at me and smiles. He pulls out a bud from one of his ears and gently puts it in mine. The lead singer shrieks the lyrics while both of us listen.

> *Don't play the game*
> *They don't set the finish line*
> *No need for shame*
> *If you try, you'll see the sign*
> *You ran the race*
> *You set the pace*
> *Win, show or place.*
> *It's all yours.*

~~~

Sam walks out onto the deck wearing nothing but a swim cap and Speedo. Most guys would look bad, very bad, in that suit. But, he looks—ahem—well, let's just say he looks like he belongs in it.

As he stands behind his platform, he pulls goggles over his head. Then he goes through a ritual of tugging the swim cap, adjusting the goggles and pressing his palms flat against them three times. He goes through this routine so many times I lose count.

Then, he rotates his arms in huge circles, shaking them. He grabs his thighs and jiggles them around until he's loose.

Flap, cap, goggles, arms one last time before he steps to the edge of the platform and bends over to dive.

My heart pounds. I'm nervous for him.

I crouch, watching him through the lens, and the official fires the gun, which startles me for a second until I find the shutter release and snap like crazy—a pic of him as he surfaces; one as he kicks; one as he makes his turn. I wish I could lie on the bottom of the pool, taking his picture as he swam above me. A dolphin's view of this event.

Sam makes the butterfly look effortless. He's almost a full length ahead when he touches the wall. *Click*. Ripping off the goggles. *Click*. Big chipped tooth grin after seeing his time. *Click*. Arms overhead for the victory shot.

Wow. Is that Sam? He looks like he could be the singer in the song. He looks like he could scream, hard and untamed, "It's all yours." This is a side of Sam he's never shown during our lunches when he's the easygoing guy who plays word games. I like it.

Even though this is new to me, it makes sense. Because if I'd thought about it before, I'd have realized he needs that streak in order to be good enough to be one of the few juniors to make it to Regionals.

And his competitive side just won him the 200-meter butterfly and a spot at the state championship. I hope Irwin's photography books taught me what I needed to know to capture Sam swimming dolphin-style.

*Streamlined in movement, dolphins possess the ability to move quickly from place to place, rapidly changing their environment. When they are in a hurry, they will jump out of the water as they reach the surface. Because it requires less energy to travel through the air than water, every leap speeds them towards their goal faster than swimming under the surface.*

*(Excerpt:* The Magic and Mystery of Dolphins*)*

# CHAPTER NINE

"We're the Fallopian Tubes," Lexie announces as I reach the water fountain the next morning.

"Huh?"

"The band. It's the new name. The Fallopian Tubes. Don't you just love it?"

No, I don't. I really, really don't. Their old name—The Ginger Girls—is so much better. It suits their music and sounds like a band that could be on the radio. I can't imagine a DJ saying, "Here's the new one from The Fallopian Tubes!" It's too weird.

But Lexie's so excited. I can't tell her it sucks, can I?

Besides, who am I to judge the name? It makes me feel a little too much like Mom. So instead of suggesting that she keep thinking up new names, I say, "That's cool. What do you want for cover art?"

Lexie's face falls. "I hadn't thought about that." Then she brightens and adds, "You'll figure it out. You're so good at that kind of thing."

She apparently has more faith in me than I do because there are no flashes of inspiration, no lightning bolts from above. In fact, this is one more thing heaped onto my rapidly growing pile of projects that include an essay for Breckenridge, helping John pack and move, homework, Mom's ever-present list, figuring out how to ask Sam to the preserve and then actually doing it and a yearbook meeting with Irwin.

Honestly, it all has me a tad stressed. Ha! Made myself laugh. A *tad* stressed. Everybody-calls-me-*Tad* Irwin. Sam would probably appreciate that, but he's hanging on to every word of a story Alana is telling. From her position in the center of the trophy case.

With lots of overly dramatic arm movements.

This makes me even crankier.

"We're gonna rehearse at Willow's later. Do you think your Mom will let you come?" Lexie asks.

"Doubtful," I say. "I've still got more than a week left on house arrest. But even if she said okay, I couldn't come. I've got a yearbook meeting and now I need to figure out what 'Fallopian Tube' artwork looks like."

Lexie's shoulders sag a little. "You don't have to do it tonight."

But I figure I better start soon before the wave of other things comes crashing down on my head.

~~~

I'm forced to skip lunch with Sam today because I need to tackle the first part of developing my photos from the Regional meet and allow three hours of drying time before finishing them after school. This doesn't improve my mood.

But if I thought *I* was stressed out and crabby, it's nothing compared to Irwin's mood. As I walk into the lab, Irwin rolls his eyes, says, "C'mon" with a huge sigh and then lumbers to the darkroom.

Once inside, everything, including Irwin, has a strange red cast to it. The smell of chemicals is overwhelming. Sharp and tangy—but not unpleasant. The area we'll work in is cramped, nothing like the open air preserve where I usually create art.

He sets to work immediately, organizing his equipment and issuing commands. "You need to measure the exact amounts for each chemical. Read the instructions on the label every single time." Or, as he picks up one container of pre-mixed chemicals,

"Here. Look. This one is about to expire. Always check the expiration dates."

The number of things to remember has my head spinning. Irwin has posted lists and rules above each step, and he taps them as he takes me through his routine. I don't love this; it's so not me.

He shows me how to agitate: invert, twist, bang, bang. Then he tells me I can find the agitation technique that works for me. Why tempt fate? I'll probably just stick with his method.

"Last year," he tells me, "Cynthia Andreade was the other photographer. The way she left the darkroom was a nightmare."

"Oh, you must be happy she graduated," I say.

"She didn't graduate. I just told Mr. Fischer I couldn't work with her anymore." Somehow this tidbit doesn't surprise me. "That's how I ended up with you." The way he says this makes me think he might prefer Cynthia.

As Irwin works, I notice he appears more confident in here than he does outside the darkroom. His fluid motions and straight shoulders make me think I could almost call him Tad.

He slowly pulls the film off the reel and clips one end to an overhead cord. "Okay, this is the last thing we'll do until after school," he says, then pulls the rest of the film off the reel and weights it with a clothes pin. Damp sponge in hand, he makes me feel the amount of water in it. "Like this," he says, sliding the sponge down the film, barely touching it. Despite his clumsiness, he does this gently, almost lovingly.

"Now you try." He hands the sponge to me. "Be careful not to scratch the negatives. They're soft right now."

I mimic his motions, treating the film as though it's something fragile in Mom's china cabinet.

"Good," Irwin proclaims. "Meet me back here after school."

We step from the darkroom into the bright fluorescent lights. His shoulders slump immediately, changing him from everybody-calls-me-Tad into plain old Irwin again.

~~~

At home that afternoon I doze, my wavy comforter snuggled under my chin. Images from school swim through my mind—Lexie in the front hall before the first bell, my meetings with Irwin. His negativity sapped my energy and left me drained. After school when we reviewed my shots of the Regional swim meet, he pointed to one after another. "Sloppy. Boring. Amateurish. Blurry. This one isn't framed right, but we might be able to save it with cropping."

Well, that was progress.

Finally we came to Sam's victory shot. It was backlit with great contrast, and the beads of water on him glistened. But the best part was his genuine smile and the emotion I captured when he raised his arms overhead. Even Irwin knew it was good.

"This is a keeper. Maybe there's hope for you yet."

I roll over and smile. The photo of Sam makes me happy, partially because it's him, and partially because I know it'll end up in the yearbook. So I accomplished one thing today. But, it's time to tackle the next project—the Fallopian Tubes cover art.

I haul myself out of bed. Sluggish. Then sit at my desk. Slowly, I flip through the sketchpad of my old ideas. What was wrong with the name Estrogen Ocean? I'd be nearly finished now.

Page turn.

I still really like the butterfly. Maybe I should hang it.

I tear this sheet from my sketchbook and set it aside.

The jellyfish are cool, but have nothing to do with Fallopian Tubes. Why did Lexie pick that as a name?

On a fresh sheet, I doodle with a sharpened pencil, tunnels, circles, the profile of a pregnant woman who could be Desiree in a couple months, the outline of a curvaceous female. I stop. And stare deeply at the drawings, which are a lot of nothing.

Then, the lightning bolt strikes.

I take the butterfly and slowly turn it upside down. What appears is a female form—and the antennae, if I angle them in rather than out, are the tubes.

This delights me more than Sam's photo. I pick up the phone and call Lexie at Willow's house where they're practicing.

Without giving her a moment to talk, I spew the idea ending with, "I'm so excited because this was everyone's favorite drawing the other day."

She whoops it up and hollers to the others, "We have cover art!" then into the phone, "I knew you'd figure it out."

Like I said, Lexie's always had more faith in me than I do. This time, it took me turning things upside down to see she was right.

~~~

After John moved into Desiree's apartment, Mom went into a cleaning frenzy. It's given our house an electrical charge, like the power lines running along the preserve where it's so quiet you can hear the crackle. That's the kind of current she's throwing off. And I don't want to get zapped.

Today she's hosing off the exterior of the house, the patio and garage floor. Dusting ceiling fan blades, the tops of doors and blinds. The linens are changed for everyone, not only John's empty room. Bathrooms sparkle; clean towels are folded and hung. Now she's armed with a toothbrush and sponge.

While dancing to the Chili Peppers, I scrub the kitchen, even though I did it two days ago. I won't complain. John told me Mom will consider time off for good behavior. With only three days left on my grounding, I plan to ask for early parole.

As I finish the floor, Mom walks into the kitchen. "This looks great. Thank you." She takes her toothbrush to a corner under the kitchen counter, loosens a few crumbs and wipes with the sponge. Cleaning is a battle to her. Today she has conquered the dirt and is gloating in victory.

Timing is everything. At least that's what John said when I asked his advice during the move to Desiree's apartment on Saturday. "You gotta catch her in just the right mood. Like when the house looks good." John carried a large box of his stuff, while I strolled next to him with an armload of clothes on hangers to the open door of the apartment. He let me go through first and said, "The bedroom's on the left."

When I walked in, it hit me—this is Desiree's room. I mean I knew they were married and everything, so I don't know what I was thinking. John would still have his own room? Duh. But still, it's a shock.

Her apartment was so different from our home. Not nearly as nice. Two bedrooms, one bath and a tiny kitchen with a stacked washer and dryer made it feel cramped. There was a weird mix of art on the walls and what Mom calls knick-knacks.

John put down the box and grinned. "Home, sweet home." He was happy to be a free man. That was his official break from Prison Robinson.

I hope to be liberated—today—by taking his advice.

"Hey, you know my grounding ends on Friday night, but a

bunch of kids from school are going ice skating tonight, so I wondered if I could go," I say while wiping the refrigerator door.

"Who's going?" she asks in a way that sounds promising. Her toothbrush attacks the kitchen faucet. At least it won't get cavities.

"Alana will be there." Mom thinks if I spend enough time with her, maybe her newfound style and popularity will polish me to a shine.

"Oh, that's great. She's beautiful on the ice."

Ack. Did she have to remind me Alana used to figure skate competitively? Instantly I feel completely inferior to my ex-bestie. "Right. Lexie's mom said she'd drive."

"Oh, Lexie's going, too?"

"Everyone's going," I say.

This is a slight exaggeration because I'd bet real money Irwin won't go. Ditto for Nigel Chang and his courtyard buddies. But there was quite a buzz at school about it, so a lot of kids will be there.

"Let me call Mrs. Murphy to make sure it's okay."

*If it makes you feel better.* "So does that mean I can go?" I ask.

"I'm confirming." Mom picks up the phone, dials, puts it to her ear and taps her fingernail on the kitchen counter, my signal to calm down.

She covers the mouthpiece. "Why don't you go dust the family room?"

*Whatever you say, Warden.*

~~~

"What size?" an old guy missing most of his front teeth says to me. He's standing behind a scarred wood counter and appears to be the official Keeper of the Skates. Capitalize that title, please.

"Eight and a half."

"No half sizes," he says, and sucks where his teeth ought to be. He grabs a pair of size nines from the shelf behind him and hands them to me.

The rink, Polar Ice, is grungy. Mom would have a conniption, because even I can see it needs a cleaning and a fresh coat of paint.

Lexie shivers, zipping her sweatshirt all the way to the top. "How did I let you talk me into this?"

I sit on the bench and pull the straps through the front of the stiff boots, snapping them into place. For some reason it reminds me of the lifejacket. Too snug. "You agreed because this is my first night of freedom in a month and you are a truly supportive friend."

"There has to be a warmer place I could support you." She waves her hand at one of the glowing red space heaters mounted to the ceiling. "A place where I don't run the risk of making a total fool of myself. I haven't done this since that scavenger hunt in middle school."

"Me either." I flip the last buckle into place and pull my hair back, twisting it into a ponytail.

Lexie jams her purse and shoes into one of the lockers, reaching for my stuff. She feeds in quarters, pulls the key and hands it to me.

I tuck it into my front pocket for safekeeping, and spy Sam walking through the automatic doorway from the public rink. He's easy to spot because he towers over everyone and doesn't wobble once as he walks on skates over to us. "Remember, I'm going to wave at you if we're talking about the Winter Ball or if I'm inviting him to the preserve. So don't skate up, okay?" I whisper.

"Yeah, yeah, yeah. You told me."

*Be cool, be cool.* I shiver and don't know if it's the rink or Sam.

"Hey Sam!" I give a dorky little wave.

That. Was. Not. Cool.

"Janey." Sam draws me into an embrace. My sweatshirt feels cozy against his sweatshirt.

"Hi Lexie," Sam says over my shoulder, still holding on. He lets go and bends over, giving Lexie a quick hug.

The three of us clump from the lobby with me as the most unsteady member of our trio. At the edge of the rink, skaters fly by at an alarming speed. Lexie steps on to the ice, pushes off hard and merges.

"Hey, I thought you said you couldn't skate," I yell at her back.

She shrugs, palms up as she nears the corner.

"Ready?" Sam asks. He steps aside to let me onto the ice first. Why is he hanging with me?

My feet slip and I windmill my arms to stay upright. Somehow I manage to keep my balance.

"I knock you off your feet." Sam laughs. He has no idea. Grasping my elbow, he steps onto the ice next to me. "Have you skated before?"

I take choppy baby steps as more experienced skaters fly by us. "Not since a scavenger hunt in seventh grade. Alana was the one who added skating to the list."

In the middle of the rink, Alana is entertaining a group of Trophy-Casers with a variety of spins. Instead of dressing like the rest of us—in jeans and sweatshirts—she's wearing black tights and a fluffy white top that looks like she's got the Easter Bunny hopping across her chest. I'm shocked Sam isn't with that crowd.

"I didn't know you used to be friends with her."

I think about this. At least he understands we aren't friends now.

"Yeah, through middle school. We hung out all the time—sleepovers and stuff. But after we got to high school I guess you could say we drifted apart. We're in different pods now, y'know?"

"Pods?" Sam asks. It's totally quiet for an extremely long, uncomfortable moment.

"That's what I call it. Like, you're in the trophy case pod because that's where you hang out when you're not in class. Lexie and I are in the water fountain pod."

"So, what do you call this when we're skating together?"

Are we skating together? Sam's much more comfortable on the skates, but his feet glide at my speed. It's nice he's going slowly for me, but I am holding him back.

"Inter-pod mingling." I laugh because it sounds so stupid.

Sam wraps his arm around my waist for a second to help me keep my balance. "You have a different way of looking at things," he says. "I hang there because Travis hangs there, and we've been friends since we munched glue sticks together. But right now, I'm hanging with you."

I try to make my feet glide the way Sam's do, but they won't cooperate. Lexie flies by me, her short blond hair ruffled by her speed. I want that kind of speed, especially tonight in my first night free from prison

"It's still inter-pod mingling," I say.

Sam snorts and rests his tongue on his chipped tooth. It's quiet until he asks, "If Eminem married John Candy?"

"Cute," I say.

We skate around and around. I try to make my feet glide

again and it works—kinda.

"You're getting it." Sam releases my elbow, and I smile at him.

My shins ache because my legs won't relax. It's hard work trying to keep your balance. The bleachers are alluring and I'd like to take a break, but don't want to leave Sam's side.

Alana flies across the middle of the rink and executes a little shoosh move to stop right in front of us. It startles me so much, I nearly fall. She grabs both of Sam's hands and skates away—backwards—pulling him from me. My equilibrium is gone.

Lexie zips up to me. "I think he's gonna ask you. I swear, Jane, the way the two of you look together, it's like you're already a couple. It's like, like you belong together."

I smile, but it's skimpy, like the outfit Alana's wearing as she skates Sam around. As they pass us, Sam lets go of her hands and grabs one of mine.

Lexie winks at me before she heads to the far end of the bleachers to hang with Lucas, Willow and Tara, who are camping out there. All along the length of the bleachers are clusters of kids: a group from the bulletin board, a group from the trophy case, even a small group from the science lab.

I wave at my water fountain friends. Lexie clasps her hands overhead in a victory move.

Oh, God. She thinks I'm giving her the signal.

Sam puts an arm around my shoulder. I lean into him; my

shins are fine now. I could skate for days. Lexie's pointing at us and doing a bootie dance. She definitely thinks we're having a vital conversation.

My internal chicken says, "Bwauck! What the cluck!" and I blurt, "Hey wanna see the place I escape to when I go all dolphin-esque? It's this cool preserve no one knows about not too far from school."

Sam's face is a question mark.

"It's really incredible. You'll feel a million miles away. There are osprey and turtles and real ducks, not warty, parking-lot ducks." I shut up before I really start blabbering.

"Sure, okay," Sam says. "When?"

What's my schedule? I hadn't thought this far ahead. "Well, I've got yearbook stuff every day except Friday. Can you do it then? After school?"

"Sounds good. A little inter-pod mingling."

Suddenly it feels like I am skating with Lexie's swiftness and Alana's poise. I can't believe it was that easy. Why did I wait so long?

# CHAPTER TEN

After Bio on Friday, Sam walks me to my locker before we head to the preserve. We pass a sign in the main hall for this year's Snow Ball.

He points. "Tickets went on sale today."

The Snow Ball is one more excuse for Trophy-Casers to mingle. As for me? I've never been.

We walk three more steps before I manage, "Are you going?" I'm not sure I want to hear the answer.

"Probably. I mean, I think so. I haven't actually asked anybody yet."

Who does he want to take? Who? *Who?* I spin the combination and try to focus on my book swap.

"It's just that the girl I want to take, um, I don't know if she'd be into—you know—the Snow Ball or stuff like that."

I pause, my hand hovering over the math text. "Why wouldn't she be?"

"Well, um, she's kinda independent and not princess-y. I mean, the Ball is formal. I'm not sure. She might think it's stupid or something." Sam's voice trails off.

Is he talking about me?

While facing him, I stuff the math book into the backpack. "I bet she's into it. I can't imagine anyone who wouldn't want to go." I hope, for a minute, I'm not boosting his confidence to ask someone else.

"That's good to know," Sam says.

I close the door and spin the lock.

We walk out the school into the blinding afternoon sunlight—a perfect day for the preserve. I reach into my backpack for a pair of sunglasses.

"Hey, Sam! Come check out my new ride," Alana leans over from the driver's seat to yell out the passenger window of a lime green Beetle. Chase stands next to the car, and Ashley sticks her head into the open passenger window.

My heart turns a green several shades darker than the Beetle. It's so unfair. Mom and Dad won't give me a car until I'm a senior. Plus, if John's car is any indication, mine will be an all-star candidate for *Pimp My Ride*.

Bagging the preserve would be the right course of action because Alana hasn't summoned me. I'm about to say, "See you Monday," but Sam grabs my elbow and steers me toward her car instead of letting me drift away.

Alana yells once more. "Sam, get in. It's so hot. My parents just bought it for me as a combo birthday-early Christmas present."

Sam smiles at me and ducks into the car. Maybe he's being polite. Inside the Bug, he's cramped—legs compressed, knees poking up. Ashley hangs in the window while I hang back.

This is a level of inter-pod mingling I hadn't expected.

Part of me wants to leave since Alana is making zero effort to include me and I feel totally out of place. But the other part wants to stay because Sam and I are going to the preserve once he's done complimenting her wheels.

The stay part wins.

Ashley covers the passenger door lock and smiles at Sam mischievously. "Ask her."

"Ask me what?" Alana gapes, blinks slowly and grips the steering wheel. She's so coy; too coy.

"Yeah, ask her what?" Sam says.

There's something about this entire scene that feels surreal—I'm having an out-of-body experience. It's really only an out-of-pod experience though, because I don't get Alana and Ashley's inside joke. What's even stranger is that it seems like Sam is confused too.

"You know, ask her."

Sam shakes his head slowly and gives Ashley, then Chase an evil eye.

"Sam wants to ask you to the dance. He's chicken," Ashley says.

*No!* That's not what's supposed to happen. He's supposed to ask me. Sam has surprise on his face and there's something else I can't quite read.

Alana reacts quickly, almost like she'd expected this to happen. "Of course I'll go with you, Sam. Why would you be afraid?"

"I wasn't." Sam glares at Chase while Alana and Ashley giggle.

The sun beats down, and I feel dizzy, like I might lose my lunch in the parking lot. I'm thankful for the sunglasses, willing myself not to cry in front of them.

Alana strokes her steering wheel. "Great. It's settled then. I'll drive."

This reminds me of the time in first grade when a kid walked up, took a lollipop out of my hand and just walked away. I couldn't believe it then, and I can't believe it's happening now.

Except this time, my lollipop is Sam.

Out of the corner of my eye, I catch a shape approaching us. It's Travis. This makes it official. What should have been one of the best afternoons—Sam and I at the preserve—has turned into one of the worst, spent in the company of my least favorite Trophy-Casers.

"What's happenin'?" Travis asks as he struts up to us.

Ashley bounces on her toes and hugs Chase. "Sam just asked Alana to the Snow Ball." Her tone declares, "isn't that just the best thing ever?"

Travis pulls his head back like he's been slapped and stares at Sam, who won't look up from his own feet. Clearly I'm not the only one out of the loop here.

I want to make my feet move but they won't, which might be a blessing. If they had, I probably would've run away.

Sam looks at Travis and lets himself out of Alana's car. "See ya'," he says to all of us, and then he takes huge, rapid strides across the parking lot like he's trampling something.

Now my feet work. "See ya," I say, hoping to catch Sam. But he moved too fast and is already crossing the street. To catch him I need to run, but I can't make myself do that.

"Hey Sam, wait up." My voice isn't loud enough, and he pulls away. Giving up, I slow my pace. The tears come.

A flash of lime green catches the corner of my eye and I hear a screech of tires. I hadn't seen the car and it barely missed me. Alana powers down the window. "Hey! Be careful Jane, I almost ran you over." She speeds off.

Almost? Isn't that exactly what happened?

~~~

Sam motions at me as I walk into the lunchroom on

Monday. A creature of habit, I get tuna and juice then slouch to our table, setting the tray down harder than I intend. He raises his eyebrows and gives me a big chipped-tooth smile as if everything is hunky dory.

I grunt and semi-smile.

"How was your weekend?" he asks.

It sucked, it sucked, it sucked. Rubbing my head to drive the thought away, I muster every bit of courage and say, "Hey, what happened on Friday?"

"Sorry. I had to get out of there. I know we were supposed to go to that preserve."

"I went anyway." I regret the words the instant they're uttered. I sound angry and bratty.

After Alana nearly squished me like a bug with her Beetle, my feet took over and led me directly to the preserve. With or without Sam I needed to go, because with my yearbook responsibilities and family stuff, I hadn't been in what seemed like forever. Once there, I went straight to the end of the dock, skipping the way I usually admire all the changes along the path. I sat and surveyed the marsh.

But the feeling of tranquility wouldn't come.

I pulled my sketchbook from the backpack and tried to capture the way the water flowed in and out of the wetlands on the far western edge. On the page, the wetlands looked spiky and sharp as spears, and the water looked solid—more like the ice rink than the preserve. Gently closing my eyes, I tilted my face toward the sky and took several deep breaths. When I opened them, black storm clouds were moving in from the west.

"I didn't stay long," I say to Sam to smooth things over. "The weather turned bad."

He nods. We eat and don't talk. In our silence I hear the clink of silverware, the hum of conversation, the sound of trays being dropped in the dishwashing chute. It's awkward, so unlike typical lunches.

Finally I say, "So you're going to the Ball with Alana, huh?"

Sam focuses on his tray, nodding. "Do you have a date yet?"

"What do you think?" I maul my tuna.

He plays with the food on his plate. "Travis wants to take you to the dance."

I stop chewing and cover my mouth as if someone has given me horrifying news about a mutual friend. In a way they have. I've spent more time with Travis this year than I want, and it's only been ten minutes here or fifteen minutes there.

"I know you don't know him very well—"

"I never said that," I explain. "He's actually the first guy I ever kissed." The *only* guy I ever kissed.

Sam's brows crease. "I didn't know you two, um, went out."

"Well, it was a long time ago—in first grade. At recess I cornered him by the jungle gym and planted a big one on his cheek."

"Lucky guy."

I swallow my sandwich, not responding because Sam just said Travis was lucky.

"He's a good person," Sam continues his pitch. "Listen, Travis doesn't have a date and neither do you. And, you are two of my most favorite people. C'mon." He gives me a puppy dog look.

"I don't think it's a good idea. I don't think we're—" I use my sandwich to push potato chips around on my plate— "compatible."

"I know, but I thought it might work out if we go together."

"Go together?"

"Yeah. We'll all go to dinner and sit together at the Ball. Travis actually wanted to take Alana and that way he can spend some time with her. And we'll get to dance together, even if I'm not Elvis and you're not Dolphin Girl."

I don't know what to say, but my heart is doing a little cha-cha. Over the weekend, after I knew Sam was not an option, I tried to think of someone, anyone at all that I'd go with and came up with only two possibilities: Nigel Chang or Brendon/Brandon—as friends only.

But Nigel's a burnout. Plus, I'd need to learn Brendon/Brandon's name to make that option work. So it seemed more likely that if I attended the Snow Ball, it'd be as a photographer for the yearbook. A witness to the winter mating ritual of Western Everglades High.

"We'll go to dinner together?"

"Alana and Ashley already picked Chez Antonio's."

"Really?" In my mind's eye, Sam and I are in this romantic, dimly lit restaurant, laughing and chatting. Alana, Travis, Ashley and Chase are only hazy images on the fringe. Taking a deep breath, I close my eyes and seal my fate. "Okay."

"You'll go with him?"

"Yes, I'll go."

"Awesome!" Sam looks like himself for the first time today. "Travis is gonna ask you, probably before the end of the day."

I don't actually share his excitement. Because even though this could be the perfect fix, the worry wart side of me is saying *what if, what if?* The answer always involves…Travis. If I'd had the freedom to choose how this all went it would have involved the preserve, a kiss from Sam and him all to myself.

# CHAPTER ELEVEN

Why does it always feel like a battle to not crumble under the force of conformity?

"Irwin, look how great these candid shots are."

"We always use group shots as the dominant photo," Irwin says for the bazillionth time as he folds his arms in front of his chest.

"I know we've always used them before, but they're boring. I know you see this. Remember how you said my swim meet shots lacked excitement?"

He relaxes a little when I say this. "It's not my call."

"I know it's not. I'm just asking you to back me on this when I present it to the page editors." Never in a million years when I agreed to take this job did I anticipate caring about yearbook layout templates. "I just think the kids who buy the yearbooks would find a photo like this—" I hold up a candid of

a service club member with his face painted like a clown—
"more interesting than this." In my other hand, I hold up a
photo of some kids sitting on the floor in front of others sitting
on chairs. Everyone's legs are angled to the right.

"You know what the kids who buy the yearbook want to
see?" His voice has turned nasty. "Pictures of themselves. That's
why we make the group photos dominant."

What's the point of arguing with him? I can't win. "Look, I
know you're comfortable with your lists and everything." I wave
at the darkroom. "But I thought you, of all people, would be a
non-conformist."

Irwin grits his teeth and looks at the floor. "We need to go
over the schedule." Candid conversation—over.

With the paper in front of us, we divvy up the assignments
for the next week. Then, in the week before Winter Break, there
are three important after-school activities: the Christmas Tree
Sale, a toy drive by the Student Government Association and the
Snow Ball.

"I'll take the tree sale and toy drive. I don't do balls." Irwin
smirks.

I laugh at first. Then a huge sigh escapes me. "Can't you do
it? Pleeeease. I'm going and don't want to take pictures all night."

"You're going? With who?" Behind the perpetually
smudged glasses I can see his eyes open in surprise.

To admit I'm going with Travis had been hard enough to

do with my water fountain friends. They all looked at me like I'd lost my mind. But I know ultimately, they still like me. Irwin's disdain will be a different matter. I can't figure out how he feels about me, but for some reason I want him to like me.

"Travis Thomlinson," I say at half volume.

Irwin pushes his glasses up the bridge of his nose and holds them in place. "Isn't he good friends with that Sam guy—the swimmer?"

Irwin might have guessed I have a thing for Sam because I've posted a couple of the swimming photos in the darkroom.

"Yeah," I say. "He's Sam Rojas' best friend. It's complicated."

A lopsided smile spreads across his face. "Okay. I'll shoot the ball, but you have to take the other two activities. Deal?"

"Deal."

~~~

Mom shoos me to the dressing room at the end of the hallway because it's large enough for both of us. Six or seven dresses weigh on my arm, and she's behind me with who knows how many more. We're over our limit, but Mom sweet-talked the sales lady.

Hanging the dresses on hooks spaced around the room, Mom oohs and aahs over her selections—all in black—so predictable. She holds a taffeta skirt. "This one is darling. Absolutely darling."

It's probably the worst of the bunch. I mean, c'mon it's taffeta.

Mom's thrilled that I'm going to the Snow Ball—and with a good boy, no less. Our shopping excursion today is the highlight of her life ever since John went and got married and moved in with Desiree. When I told her I'd been asked, she said, "Oh honey, you're blooming, even if it is a little late."

What she doesn't realize is it took a lot of fertilizer to get me here. I'm going with Travis Thomlinson, for God's sake.

And even that seemed up in the air for a while because he didn't ask until four days after my conversation with Sam. But he did. Finally. And I, according to the plan, said yes.

This is the fourth store we've hit, and I'm firm on leaving here with a gown. I'm sick of shopping, sick of Mom. And since we can't agree on anything—not style, not color, not length—it's time for me to make a stand.

"I really want something unique. Something that says Jane, Jammin' Junior," I tell her. That sounds pretty dorky, but she always riles me up.

"I want you to look beautiful too, honey. Nothing says sophistication like a little black dress." Mom sorts the gowns in the order she wants me to try them. She pauses, surveying one with teeny rhinestones circling a halter neckline and holds it in front of me. "Oooh, so cute."

"All the girls will be wearing black and for once, just once in my life, I want to stand out and be noticed. Can't you understand?"

I take one of my choices—a pale aqua mermaid dress—off its hanger and shimmy into it. Mom clucks her tongue while I turn sideways for her to fasten the hook at the back.

In the three-sided mirror I toss my head side to side, feeling elegant. "I like this one." It's glidy and floaty. It's me.

Mom rubs her hand gently across her forehead, studying my reflection and taps her forefinger on the wall. "I adore that cut on you, but the color is all wrong for this time of year. It's too bright. It's meant to be a prom dress."

What difference does the color make if I feel pretty?

"My favorite's the black feathered dress at Gowns Galore," she continues. "It was very chic."

Chic, Schmeek! It had feathers. I wonder if she's from another planet because her favorite would make me look like a crow.

I pose in the aqua gown, doing my best to sell her. "This is the one."

"You haven't even tried on the others."

Twirling in the mermaid gown, I say, "I love this."

"Just try them. Maybe you'll find something better."

Why fight it?

One by one, I slip into and out of the gowns; zip, snap, tie, fluff. I'm a Winter Ball Barbie doll clothed in rich jewel hues of burgundy, royal purple, evergreen and black and black and black.

The sales lady knocks on the door. "How're you doing in there?"

Mom opens the door a crack. "We only have a few more to try."

"Let me know if I can help," she says, and I hear her carpeted footsteps fade away.

Two dresses are left, both black, including the one with rhinestones Mom deemed "oh-so cute." The dressing room is oppressively small.

"I don't need to try these on. I can tell I don't like them."

"What about this?" Mom holds the skirt of the rhinestone dress.

"It's boring," I practically yell at her.

"Honey, this dress is not boring, it's classic. And see, the bottom is quite interesting." She points out the hem of the dress is longer in back and uneven. I clench my teeth. There's no way she's getting me into that dress and she senses it. "Okay. Try on the aqua dress again."

Burying a smug smile, I slip into my favorite. I see the finish line, and I'm going to win this time. Mom fastens the neck hook, and I'm surrounded by my reflection. This dress is perfect. It's exactly what Dolphin Girl should wear.

The saleslady knocks again. Mom throws open the door, which is a teeny bit embarrassing.

"I love that dress on you," the saleslady says. "A lot of people have tried it on, but they never buy it." She tugs at the waist, making a minor adjustment.

"Why not?" Mom asks like she's concerned it's defective.

"Because of this." The saleslady bends over and grabs the bottom where it flares out. "See, if you hem this dress, you lose the line. But—" she holds me at arms' length— "it's made for you."

There's love and enthusiasm in her voice. Either it really is made for me, or she's an excellent saleslady.

"Plus, since nobody's been the right height, it's marked down." She pulls the tag under my arm and shows Mom. I see slashes of red, blue and purple ink. "You want it?" The sales lady is definitely an advocate for my gown.

Mom rubs her chin. "I think we have a few more to try. Thanks." She closes the door and pushes the lock.

"Aw, Ma."

"Humor me, Jane." She takes the black halter dress on the hanger and holds it right under my chin. "See, sophistication, right?" Then, she moves it away so I'm in the aqua dress. She does the gesture again.

The black dress is more elegant. God, I hate it when she's right.

"So you want me to try this one?" I resign myself to doing what she wants, realizing the nightmare is not over.

"I think so. I know you see it. You have an artist's eye." She says this gently, taking away some of the sting.

I slip into the silky dress, which is just this simple halter, low cut, super tight under my chest and cut sort of A-line with a wide bottom. Mom gets behind me to hook the neck and looks over my shoulder at me in the mirror.

"Oh, honey." Her eyes tear.

Mine are a little watery too, because this stupid dress was nothing special on the hanger, but now it looks pretty good. It clings in all the right spots and there's a glow, a clear aura framing me. It must be the rhinestones.

"Look. It's the perfect length," Mom says.

The bottom of the gown breaks at my arch. I glance over my shoulder at my back and it looks good from that direction, too. It's world's better than the taffeta one, galaxies better than the feathers.

I know this dress is similar to what other girls will wear, but for a minute I feel like I could fit into the trophy case crowd and become one of them. If just for one night.

And so I weigh my options—blend, or be myself? It's not as easy you'd think. I take another peek in the mirror. I look nice in this dress. I glance at the aqua gown and try to choose.

Mom makes the decision for me. She hugs me from behind,

kisses me on the cheek and beams. "You're going to look beautiful. Take it off, and I'll go pay for it while you get dressed." While I slip out of the dress she adds, "We still need to get you shoes and a purse, and something pretty for your hair." Mom lifts my hair at the back of my head. I sigh and she adds, "Maybe another day."

She leaves me alone to get dressed. In the three-way mirror, I glimpse my dolphin tattoo as I slip into my jean shorts. It scolds me. I'm not a little-black-dress person. This day has been one big battle—and, of course, Mom fashioned the outcome.

Before leaving the dressing room, I take the mermaid gown from the hook and hold it in front of me, turning this way and that. The saleslady's face appears behind me. "Oh, I'm glad you decided on that one."

"I'm not getting—" I start to tell her about the black dress, but say then instead, "Could you hold this for me? For one day?"

She smiles and takes the hanger from me. "Sure thing, hon. It's made for you."

*In the wild, bottlenose dolphins can be seen playing with articles, like stones or sponges, found in their habitat. Sometimes they drape seaweed on their heads or bodies and resemble nothing so much as little girls playing a game of dress-up.*
*(Excerpt:* The Mystery and Magic of Dolphins*)*

# CHAPTER TWELVE

Rodeo Bob's is lit up with a neon cowboy being kicked by a neon jackass. Oops, I mean donkey. Every time the donkey kicks, the cowboy's neon hat flies off.

How have I ended up here?

My three-inch silver sandals click-clack on the unfinished, hardwood floors. The lobby is decorated in early cattle drive; the speakers blare with the same music Travis played in his pickup on our way here.

I turn to Travis. "You said the food's good here?"

"Huh?" He leans closer, his ear to my mouth. I can see the top of his head.

When we bought my shoes, I moaned they would make me too tall. Mom's advice: Don't be afraid of your height. With Sam, they would have been fine.

"The food's good here?" I yell.

"You're right—it's hard to hear." A tuxedoed Travis slips his arm around my waist, oblivious to the fact that we look totally out of place.

It's hard to miss me in my rhinestone gown as I wobble to an open spot, scanning for a place to sit. Unfortunately, we're trapped like roped rodeo sheep.

A lady in blue jeans, cowboy boots and a western shirt stands next to me. It's not my style, but at least she's dressed for Rodeo Bob's. She turns to her boyfriend, who's also dressed cowboy. "Isn't that cute? It must be their prom or sumthin'."

*Or sumthin'* is more like it.

Earlier tonight, I hid out in Mom's dressing area because in every single TV show or movie I've seen, the girl makes an "entrance." Quotation marks, please. This way I could walk downstairs while Travis gazed up at me, spellbound, from the first floor.

Honestly, it seemed phony. If I were going with Sam, I'd probably open the front door myself.

Mom poked her head in to check on me. "Look what I've got," she said, waving a rhinestone hairclip. We'd searched high and low for something to pull up my hair—with no luck. "I found it yesterday."

I perched on the upholstered bench in front of her vanity while she fiddled with the back of my head.

"Beautiful. Look." She handed me a mirror, and I angled it to see the clip. Perfect.

Mom and I have reached some kind of truce since the invitation to the ball. At times during our shopping expeditions, I wanted to shoot her, or better yet, myself. But she honestly wanted to help, and our ceasefire has lasted more than a week.

Maybe this is the mother-daughter relationship she always wanted. Or maybe I became the good child, what with John's new life and everything.

I stood and slipped into the sandals while Mom compulsively smoothed the back of my dress. "If some of the kids go out after the dance, you can go, but be sure to call and let us know. Don't go off by yourself. And if someone offers you alcohol, don't take it."

Her advice and the de-wrinkling bugged me, but I knew she meant well, so I hugged her and said, "I know. Don't worry, Mom."

When the doorbell chimed, she said, "That's probably Travis. I'll go downstairs and—Wait! One more thing." She dashed to her jewelry box and returned a moment later with her diamond pendant and fastened it at the back of my neck. "There. Now you're ready."

We did the pin-the-flower-take-the-photo-shake-the-hand-be-careful-and-have-fun-thing in the entry hall. In the pickup on the way to the restaurant, Travis announced there'd been a change of plans and that we were going to Rodeo Bob's, home of the best steak and ribs.

"Oh, I thought we were going to Chez Antonio's," I said.

Travis impatiently pushed a button to get the CD to a track he wanted to hear. "Sam likes to call all the shots."

"Oh. Yeah." I sorta giggled and played along. "So he likes Rodeo Bob's?"

"*I* like it. Chez Antonio is too stuffy."

I was totally confused. "So, Sam and Alana are meeting us there? I mean, at Rodeo Bob's?"

"No, I called the shots this time. We'll see them at the dance." He paused. "Maybe."

"Oh." I was like a broken record of vowel sounds—oh, oh, oh. It sounded like I was at a loss for words, but not so. I just couldn't say aloud all the words in my head: *What about Sam? You didn't take Alana here for a formal, did you? What about Sam? I can't believe he's going to have dinner without me. I really wanted to try the food at Chez Antonio's. What about Sam?*

I might have gone on like this all the way to the restaurant if Travis hadn't interrupted my thoughts. "You ever been to Rodeo Bob's?"

"No," I confessed.

"Well, besides havin' the best steak and ribs, they give you a bucket of peanuts in the shell, and you get to throw the shells on the floor. It's great."

As we stand in this crowded lobby, I try to avoid the peanut shells on the floor and play with Mom's diamond pendant. Who knew she'd let me wear her favorite necklace? Guilt creeps in— when we get to the dance, I'm switching into my aqua mermaid gown, courtesy of Lexie. This dress isn't me, but neither is the restaurant, so I guess it doesn't matter.

Thank God our wait for a table is brief and the waitress seats us in the back. As she hands us oversized cow-shaped menus, I notice her nametag says *Howdy! I'm Betty Lou*, which I don't believe for a minute.

The table's good—we're out of view, and now I have something to hide behind. Reading it, or pretending to, gives me an excuse for not talking to Travis. *I want to hug you, Betty Lou, or whatever your real name is.*

Travis lowers the cow and peeks at me. "Know what you're havin'?"

"Still looking. How about you?"

"The baby back ribs." Travis helps himself to some peanuts, cracks them open and munches away. He throws the shells to the floor and pushes the bucket toward me. "Here, eat some."

I would have figured out Travis was a peanut fan even if he hadn't told me, because our bucket is almost half empty now and

I'm still playing with my first one as I scan the menu. I've never been a carnivore and the menu screams beef, pork and chicken. The only fish is fried catfish. I bet Chez Antonio's has awesome seafood.

Once I settle on the Shrimp Ka-RODEO-Bob's, I can't use entree selection to avoid Travis any longer. I fold the menu, plastering a pleasant, interested expression on my face.

Travis smiles at my boobs. "Didya' decide?"

"The shrimp kabobs sound good." I gingerly place the peanut shell next to my water glass and Travis brushes it to the floor.

"You should have the ribs. You don't know what you're missing."

I don't like ribs.

During the awkward silence that follows, I take my napkin and polish my silverware. Then I polish Travis's silverware. Suddenly I realize this is prissy behavior, like something Mom would do. I stop, fold the napkin and lay it on my lap.

Sam and Alana must be huddled close, sipping designer water with floating lemon slices, while Travis belches his root beer. Strolling violinists serenade them while we groove to "Red Neck Woman." They're enjoying candlelight, while I bask under barn-themed fixtures.

I so want this dinner to end.

Unfortunately, the rest of the meal is more of the same.

Travis wolfing his food and licking sticky barbeque sauce from his fingers. Me, elevating to a whole new level of prissiness I would have thought impossible. Could it be this dress? I even hand him a Wet Nap to wipe his hands. The worst part is when Travis says, "Sam did a good thing, fixin' us up."

"Yeah?" I ask in confusion. Because this *date*—and I use that word tongue in cheek—was not the plan. Wasn't Travis supposed to be with Alana? Wasn't Sam supposed to be with me? Weren't we supposed to be eating much better food?

"Yeah. Now you can stop hangin' out at the water fountain. What do you see in those kids anyway?"

I grab a handful of peanuts and viciously crack one open. "I like them."

"As if." Travis guffaws.

It's the most awkward moment in an evening filled with them. Finally, Betty Lou whisks our plates away. No more silverware to polish, no more peanuts to crack, so I arrange the salt, pepper and barbeque sauce, giving my date a tight smile.

Travis smiles back. "Sam always says how cool you are." His foot taps my leg.

"Sorry," I draw my leg away. "Yeah, I think Sam's pretty cool, too." A minute later I sense his shoe again and pull my legs under the picnic bench seat. "It's okay. He told me you really wanted to go with Alana."

Travis' socked-foot returns, slowly sliding along my calf

under the silky gown. "I did, but maybe everything worked out for the best." He rubs his foot along the inside of my thigh.

Omigod! This is no accidental kick. This is footsie.

Travis is giving me some kind of dreamy, half-lidded, sexy-stud look. Either that or he's sleepy.

*Ewwww.*"Um, uh—I've got to go to the little girl's room," prissy-me says.

I hop up and do a combination hobble-jog to the bathroom. *Crunch.* I look down. There's a peanut shell stuck on my heel. *Just keep going.* I bang open the heavy wood door that reads Fillies. When the door swings shut behind me, I turn and press my forehead into the cool concrete wall. I wish I could call Lexie, but I left my cell in the bag at the table.

"That bad, honey?" The cowgirl from the lobby leans over the sink, her face close to the mirror, and lipsticks her mouth. She blots the excess on a toilet paper square.

I nod, pulling the peanut shell off my heel.

"Is that your guy?" she asks.

I don't know how in the world to explain to her that my guy set me up with this guy. It sounds ridiculous, even to me, and I'd agreed to it.

I wash my hands and grab a paper towel from the dispenser. The cowgirl and I are the only ones in the Rodeo Bob's bathroom. "It's not really my guy," I explain. "It's a first date.

"Those can be awkward."

"No, what I mean is—it's my first date—ever."

She gives me a friendly pat on my upper arm. "They get easier. It'll get better. Relax."

"Are you sure?" I can't imagine it getting any worse, but I don't believe her either. This is Travis we're talking about.

"Can't get any worse than hiding in the bathroom, right?" she says with an infectious giggle that makes me giggle back. "Good luck, sweetie." She pats my arm again and leaves.

Staring at my reflection in the mirror, it dawns on me that the critter in the neon sign isn't a donkey but a jackass, as I first thought. I'm the jackass, and Travis is the cowboy. How could it be anything else? Only a jackass would end up at Rodeo Bob's for a dance, kicked by a cowboy attempting footsie. Only a jackass would run to the bathroom to hide.

For a moment I imagine myself kicking Travis, my cowboy-date, just like the Rodeo Bob's sign. But it's only my imagination, not something I would ever do. Maybe the cowgirl was right. It'll get better. I boldly return to the table, sit in front of my dessert and make small talk to pass the time. Travis doesn't try his moves again. Soon we'll be at the dance, sitting with Sam.

I decide she's right—it has to get better.

# CHAPTER THIRTEEN

The ballroom at the Signature Grand is practically empty when we walk in. "I guess we're early," Travis says.

The decorating committee did an incredible job. The snowflake-themed hall glistens. White puffy pom-poms hang from the ceiling, and opalescent icicles adorn each table. If I hadn't been so busy with my yearbook job, I would have helped.

The AC is set as low as it will go, so the room will stay cool when everybody gets here. But right now it's freezing in a Snow Ball kinda way. I shiver, and Travis puts his arm around my shoulder.

He leads me to a small table for two along the back wall. Here, we'll be tucked away, removed from the action. There's not much to do in our little corner of the world, and we exhausted every possible conversation at the restaurant. Travis taps his toes and drums the table to the music while I scan the room, only finding Irwin.

He hugs the far wall, a camera slung around his neck, sipping Snow Ball punch from a clear plastic cup. His attire is interesting: black jeans, black sneakers and a T-shirt printed to look like the front of a tuxedo. I'm not sure if he's trying to fit in or if he's mocking us, but either way he's a lot less rumpled than most days.

Couples trickle in and eventually stream through the front doors, and while I'm on the lookout for Sam or Lexie, I see Alana. She's wearing my dress. I mean, it's her dress, but it's exactly the same as mine, right down to the rhinestones surrounding the neckline. It's no surprise she looks better than I do.

Sam, Ashley and Chase follow her like Academy Award nominees strutting on the red carpet. They grab a big table near the dance floor. Alana plops her beaded bag on top and waits for Sam to pull out her chair. But Sam misses this cue because he's watching Travis and me. He motions for us to come join them while Alana rolls her eyes and huffs.

"You don't want to go over, do you?" Travis shakes his head, answering for me.

I stand and cringe inwardly. "If I'm going to hang with you guys I probably need to get to know everybody." Before he can object I walk away.

Left with no other option, he follows.

Sam pulls out the chair for Alana and then pulls out the chair on the other side of him for me.

Alana, her eyes and mouth a phony crinkle, says, "Jane. Nice dress."

Thank God I'm changing when Lexie gets here.

~~~

The seating and the company at this table makes me feel more confined than when I was under house arrest. Although my gown blends, I don't.

Alana and Ashley's conversation has been a tour of the mall and shopping. The only time I was included was when Ashley asked me where I got my gown.

"The bridal shop at Broward and Seventieth," I replied.

"That's where I got mine," Alana said. She propped her elbow on the table and used her hand as a shield as she talked to Ashley, not even making an attempt to hide the fact that she was talking about me.

That had stung. What made me think they'd be nice tonight? Travis is busy talking to Chase about some ESPN special. While I have only been snubbed for a couple of minutes, it feels like hours of rejection.

I don't know what possesses me—maybe just a need for human interaction—when I turn to Sam and say, "If Coco

Chanel married Geoffrey Beene—"

Sam snorts, smacks the table and turns bright red. I'm laughing along with him, so happy he liked this one, until I see everyone's confused expression. My laughter dies fast.

Sam says, "It's this game. So, if Coco Chanel married Geoffrey Beene, she'd be Coco Beene. Get it?"

Travis shrugs. Ashley executes an eye roll so perfect, if she was in competition it'd earn a perfect ten.

But Sam enjoys it, and when he turns and says, "Good one," Alana clasps his shoulder from behind and pulls him backwards, saying, "Do you want some punch?" She means *she* wants some punch—or, more likely, she wants Sam away from me.

He obliges, taking Travis and Chase with him. I'm left alone with Alana and Ashley. Between the dress and the company, I feel like a fish out of water.

Where's my pod?

Lexie bursts into the ballroom, immediately waving and motioning me over. I turn to the girls. "I'll be back."

"Yeah. Catch up with us later," Alana says. Two years ago it would have sounded like *hurry back* but now it sounds like *whatever*.

I do a wobble-jog to the bathroom, using it as my escape for the second time tonight. What are the odds of that? Once there, my heels clickety-click against the tile and echo off the ceramic fixtures.

"Ooh, thank you, thank you." I hug Lexie. Taking the garment bag from her, I make my way to the largest stall at the end, hanging the bag from the top of the door. I leave the door cracked open so we can talk, and shimmy out of the black halter dress.

"You know, Jane, most people would've just changed at my house."

"I'm not most people." I remove the pale gown from the hanger and toss it over my head. "Besides, my mom would have never let Travis pick me up somewhere else."

Lexie laughs.

"Where'd you go for dinner?" I try to reach the zipper in back.

"Willow's mom decided at the last minute to serve food on their patio. Their house is beautiful. The sun was going down. It was really nice."

That does sound nice. Not as fancy as Chez Antonio's, but a big step up from my dinner.

"How was Chez Antonio's?" Lexie asks. I might hear envy in her voice.

"I have no idea." I step out of the stall. "Zip me, please." I look over my shoulder. "Travis took me to Rodeo Bob's. Don't ask."

"No way." Lexie giggles. Yeah, I'd probably laugh too if it

hadn't happened to me.

I spin around. The gown swirls out at the bottom.

"Aw. You look beautiful. The other dress was nice, but that looks more you." She gives me a hug. "Here. I have something else for you." She unzips a pocket on the garment bag and pulls out a necklace. "When I saw this, I thought of you. It'll look perfect with that dress."

It's this really cool necklace with seashells and pearls all jumbled together.

"It's awesome!" Because she's shorter than me, I bend at the knees so she can hook it. Lexie's dolphin necklace conceals Mom's beautiful pendant, letting me honestly be me. Then, I grab the garment bag from the hook and hand Mom's dress to her.

Lexie zips it. "Mission Number One completed—now for Mission Two."

"What's that?"

She smiles like she's got a secret. "We've got The Fallopian Tubes' gear in Lucas' dad's van."

"You didn't tell me they said okay. The last I'd heard, the Snow Ball committee said no set."

"So," she says, "why would that stop me? We'll both make our debut—me as a singer, and you in that amazing gown. Let's go."

Surveying myself in the mirror, the gown is totally me, but

now fear grips me because I'm heading back into foreign territory. I squeeze her wrist. "I'm so out of place at that table. First date. Sixteen. Never been kissed. It's pathetic. I bet I'm the only person here who hasn't been kissed."

"Uh, Travis. First grade."

"That doesn't count, and you know it." I stare into Lexie's eyes.

"You don't know that. I bet there's someone else who hasn't," she says.

"Who?"

She gets a twinkle in her eye. "Irwin?"

I shake my head. "Thanks. That's exactly what I mean."

She puts her arm around my shoulder and gives me a hug. "You'll get kissed. Everyone does."

"I don't see how."

"C'mon, you will. Sam said he'd dance with you." Lexie nudges out the bathroom door, which has soundproofed us from what was going on at the Ball.

The DJ screams, "Shake it" to Outkast, and the dancers follow his instructions. There's shaking, grinding, and one couple simply needs to go get a room. I mouth *pathetic* to Lexie, but she aims me towards the trophy case table and gives me another push.

~~~

Irwin looks through the lens. "I can't see Travis." He tried to set us up as boys in the back row, girls in the front, but it's not working because Travis is the same height as me with these heels. "Alana, switch with Jane," he says.

She makes a face but does it anyway, because she wants this photo to make it into the yearbook.

"Much better," Irwin says, and right before he takes the first picture, Sam grabs me around the waist and pulls me back against him.

Ooh la la!

"Take a few more," I tell Irwin, and Sam holds me close while he snaps away.

Then, Travis, Chase and Sam pose as body-builders while Alana and Ashley act like fashion models, hands on hips, lips pursed, tossing their heads to and fro.

Travis seizes Alana and whispers in her ear.

Finally Irwin says, "Thanks, guys. I'm off to find the next yearbook victims." As he strolls away, Travis grabs Alana by the hand and pulls her onto the dance floor.

It's my chance.

But before I can make my move, Sam extends his hand. "Dance?" He doesn't wait for my answer, guiding me to a spot far away from Travis and Alana. We dance around to "Be My Girl?" by Jet. It's not easy to dance to, sort of a herky-jerky rhythm.

Sam knows every word, sings the whole song. Every time he says "Are you gonna be my girl?" I want to scream *yes, yes, yes* but don't even know if he's asking me the question or just singing along. As the song ends the DJ puts on a slow number. Kids move on and off the dance floor with the new selection, and we're stuck in the flow of traffic. I wish he would have asked me to dance to this one.

"Thanks. That was fun," I say.

Sam holds my hand. "One more?"

*Oh!* I can't believe he asked me. "Sure," I say all nonchalant like this happens all the time.

He pulls me close, and I cuddle, resting my head on his shoulder, nestled against his chin. His neck is part cologne, a hint of sweat, and mostly Sam. I inhale. We barely move in slow, little circles, hardly dancing. It's more like a very long hug. I think I'm melting and wonder if we can stay this way for the rest of the night.

He whispers in my ear, "You always surprise me."

"Huh?" Not your most articulate response.

"You look so different in that dress."

Aaah. Now I know what this is about. The dress change. Why'd *she* have to buy the same dress?

"Oh, you mean different from Alana. Well, I always wanted this dress, but my mom wanted the other."

Sam leans his head away from me but keeps the rest of his

body close. He stares me straight in the eye. "You look different from her, but that's not what I meant. I meant, you look different from the girl I eat lunch with every day. You look incredible tonight. "

He doesn't wait for a reply, embracing me instead. I mumble "thanks" into his neck, as close to a kiss as I've ever come. We cuddle and turn more small circles. I'm not even sure if my feet are touching the dance floor. Is this what it feels like to be high, everything slow-moving and surreal?

I don't want this dance to end. Can't I stay in this cocoon a while longer?

~~~

I take a small sip of the spiked Snow Ball punch when Lexie buzzes by, poking me in the waist. "Time to boogie!" She rushes over to the DJ and as she talks to him, waves her arms around and then clasps them like she's begging. The next thing I know, they're setting up amps, mics and instruments. Somehow Lexie convinced him to let her play.

The DJ grabs the mic and says, "And now, for your listening pleasure, The Fallopian Tubes!"

Willow tugs a rope, and a small banner with my inverted butterfly artwork unfurls at the front of the stage. Lexie yells into the mic, "Are you ready?"

The water fountain table goes nuts, the science lab table laughs and my table rolls their eyes and keeps talking.

I stand, whooping and clapping. Travis gives me an *are you nuts?* look, but Sam stands and claps along with me.

The Tubes open with a cover of "Walk Like An Egyptian", an old Bangles song—now that's a good girl band name—and Lexie sounds great. They all do. She starts the funky Cleopatra walk we all practiced in Willow's garage. "C'mon everyone," she yells into the mic, but the dance floor is empty.

I walk to the middle and do an Egyptian strut, around and around, laughing at Lexie. What's gotten into me? Dancing on the floor Egyptian-style is almost like an item we'd put on one of our hunts, and that makes it even better. Over at my table Sam's laughing, snorting, going red in the face, but Travis looks mortified and Alana looks smug. Willow breaks from drumming and uses her sticks to strike the pose in both directions and then smashes the cymbals at just the right time.

A couple of people join me. There's probably ten of us having fun on the floor when the song ends.

For the next number, they perform an original—Sweet Temptation. Nobody knows this one so the dance floor empties except for me waving my hands slowly over my head because it's sort of ballad-y. I don't even bother to look at my table. Who cares?

The Tubes play at least another five songs. Everyone is into it and they could keep going, but I can tell they won't get the chance because Jordan Wilson, ruler of all things WEHS—including this dance—is annoyed and giving the DJ a hard time. He shrugs and lets Lexie know one more with a raised index finger. I sorta wish she'd send back a different message by using another finger, but she nods and closes with Pink's "Raise Your Glass." It's the perfect message for Jordan. Now, if only she would.

I'm groovin' on the crowded floor when all of sudden I notice Sam bouncing next to me.

"Are you?" he asks.

"Am I what?"

"Wrong in all the right ways?"

I look up at Lexie. She's moving with abandon around the stage. I wish I could move like that. Then I look at how full the dance floor is and through the crowd, I see Irwin at the edge of the floor. He's snapping pictures and in between each focus, he does a little move. It's barely noticeable, just for himself. Then he lifts his plastic cup of Snow Ball punch like he's toasting me.

"Yeah, I am," I say to Sam, "And, I'm having a blast."

~~~

Back at the table, after Lexie's performance and my boogie, I'm shunned. Alana and Ashley are hunched together talking, and it's like I'm invisible. I can't understand why she isn't excited for Lexie. "Remember how Lexie always talked about this during our sleepovers?" I ask her.

"Yeah." She smiles.

Her genuineness encourages me. "Remember the time Lexie fell asleep and we froze her bra and she put it on for us the next morning and ooh-oooh'd all around?" I laugh, and Sam does too.

Ashley barks one hard, "Ha."

Alana's expression makes me feel like she's looking down on me. And I'm six inches taller than her. "That was pretty immature, huh?"

It was funny. *You thought so, too.*

There's a tap on my back. I turn around to see Irwin hovering over my shoulder, a sick expression on his face.

"What's wrong?" I ask.

"Jane, can I talk to you for a minute? Outside?" He heads off without waiting for an answer.

I don't even bother to apologize or make excuses to anyone else, but I whisper to Sam, "I'll be back." Then I hurry outside.

Irwin's hunched over by shrubbery at the edge of the parking lot, puking.

I walk up and rub his back in circles. "It's okay. You're gonna be okay. Didn't you know the punch was spiked?"

Irwin wipes his mouth with his hand and stares at me with

scared eyes through the dirty glasses. "The punch was spiked?" His face looks incredibly young.

"Here." I gently lift the camera over his neck. "I'll take the pictures. I bet you got most of the good stuff already." Pulling my cell from the small jeweled bag, I say, "Want to call your mom?" I glance at the hand he just used. "I'll dial for you."

His face crumples, and he sits hard on the curb, resting his head on his knees. "I can't call her. She'll kill me. I mean, really kill me." Then he starts crying.

That's not good. Irwin can't be seen like this. He'll never live it down.

On top of that, I'm at loss. This strikes me as so odd, because here's this guy who's extremely independent. He doesn't care what anyone thinks, acts just as he pleases, and he's worried about his mom. I mean, I worry about my mom, but I worry about everyone.

Flipping open the phone, I search my contacts for John and push send. After all, he said to call if I need anything.

The phone rings twice, and John picks up. "Everything okay?"

It's nice that he's worried—I hope he's all right with my request.

"Yeah, I'm fine. But, a friend of mine isn't. Remember Irwin, the other photographer? I think he needs a ride home."

*When an adolescent male dolphin identifies a female he's interested in, he'll exhibit many flashy behaviors to capture her attention. If that's not successful, he'll work to separate her from her pod.*
*(Excerpt:* The Magic and Mystery of Dolphins*)*

# CHAPTER FOURTEEN

The pickup is silent, and it's a blessing not to have to listen to country.

"Wanna cruise by the beach?" Travis suddenly asks.

I'm stunned. I was sure he wanted to dump me at home and then meet up with everyone else there. I mean, after Irwin got sick I spent the night taking yearbook pictures. We never even danced together.

"Do ya?"

"Okay." I fidget with my bag. Maybe-possibly-somehow we'll run into Sam?

As he drives, Travis rolls down the windows. The air expands as soon as we cross over US-1. Once we pass over the bridge at the Intracoastal, I can smell the ocean calling to the dolphin in me.

"There they are." Travis points to a group in gowns and tuxedoes standing around a small bonfire at the edge of the basketball courts. All the parking spaces are full, so Travis drives up the beach until he finds an open spot.

Before I climb down from the truck, I slip out of the silver sandals, glad to be rid of them. Then I bunch the dress so it won't drag on the ground. But as soon as my toes touch the cool, damp sand, I decide to let it go. A breeze swirls the flared mermaid bottom.

There are a lot of faces I recognize around the beach bonfire: Ashley, Chase, Whitney, Alex, even Karen Perry—but Sam and Alana aren't here yet. When we join the pod, Travis high-fives his buddies and then goes into his d-bag routine. This time he's doing a tribal dance. More than any other time tonight, I feel trapped.

I wander away from the trophy case cluster and immediately feel lighter.

Along the shore, gentle waves lap at the bottom of my dress, which drags along behind me picking up sand and seaweed. Staring out across the water, a full moon reflects on a violet ocean, creating a sensation of déjà vu. It's like the sketch I did for Lexie's band with one difference. Out past the sand bar, I see movement. Two dorsal fins break the surface and circle each other.

Amazing—dolphins.

*We're here.*

I turn around to see who said that, but the group still stands around the bonfire. Their voices are too distant, and the conversation they're having sounds like birds chattering.

Now the surface of the ocean is glassy, unbroken. I must have imagined them. The ocean lulls me into a trance until someone stands behind me, hands on my waist.

"The dance was cool," Travis says, breaking the spell.

"Yeah. Thanks for asking me."

He puts a hand on my waist and guides me along the edge of the water. "Do you remember kissing me on the playground?"

The atmosphere is romantic. If my life were a storybook romance this would have been awesome. The guy I kissed in first grade taking me to my first high school dance and ending the evening with a walk on the beach. How perfect is that? But alas, my life is as messy as my bedroom.

"I bet you're a better kisser now," Travis says.

*Don't bet on it.* A foolish gamble.

I don't know what to say or do. I'd imagined every part of the dance: Chez Antonio's, the hall, dancing with Sam, but hadn't anticipated a walk on the beach with Travis. In fact, I hadn't thought post-dance at all.

He leans in and closes his eyes. He wants a kiss.

Travis might not be the last person I'd kiss, but he might be. Sam would be my first choice, but can I continue to be choosy? Once you've gone sixteen years without one, it'd be easy to make it to twenty or thirty. Can you say Old Maid?

I glance back at the group huddled down the beach. There's still no sign of Sam or Alana. He's probably kissing her right now.

Never kissed. Does that make me unlovable? It's not like there's been all these great opportunities with Sam. Or anyone else, for that matter. If I let this chance slip away, who knows when another guy will even try?

*You can pretend he's Sam,* I tell myself. Think of it as practice for the real thing.

I place my hands on Travis' face and meet his soft lips. His tongue darts and thrusts between my lips, and I do the same.

Am I doing this right? It doesn't feel right.

Travis' mouth has engulfed mine and his tongue is halfway down my throat. I try to think *Sam, Sam, Sam,* but it doesn't work. Finally he breaks away.

Does that count? Is that it, my real first kiss?

"Nice," Travis whispers. "Better than first grade."

I glance over his shoulder at the group around the bonfire. Where's Sam? I wish it didn't matter who I was kissing, wish that I felt free enough to kiss anyone. There's probably some rule for the trophy case pod about not dating inexperienced girls. I don't mean an official rule, more like something everyone knows—even Sam.

If I get better at this, maybe it'll make me more attractive to Sam. Maybe when I get my chance, I'll knock him off his feet.

Travis is facing me, holding onto both my hands. Since I'm barefoot, he's slightly taller. I tilt my face and kiss him, thoughts swirling through my head.

This isn't as fun as I thought.

He kisses my neck, my ears and the thoughts won't stop.

Do I feel different now that I'm kissed?

Without breaking away, Travis pulls me to the sand.

Would Sam do that? Is he kissing Alana? Why didn't he come?

I can't stop thinking about Sam, and these kisses are as phony as my stairway entrance. If I were kissing Sam, I wouldn't be able to think at all.

Realizing this isn't what I want, I stop, but it doesn't faze Travis. In fact, he's pushing me to lie on the sand.

I press back.

He gives one hard shove, and my head thumps against the sand.

"Ow," I grab the back of my head.

Travis stops and places his hand over mine and gently rubs the sore spot. "Sorry," he says and laughs. I don't think he is. "Show me your ink. That dolphin is delish."

Delish? Seriously? He's so cheesy. "We should go." The sand has dampened my dress and my mood.

But Travis kisses my neck again, cups his hand over my breast and moans. He nuzzles his head down to my chest. *Oh, God! This has to stop.*

"No," I squeak.

Travis removes his hand but kisses me again on the lips. He's positioned himself on top of me and I'm pressed into the sand, my voice and movement cut off.

I thrash my head to the side. "I mean it, Travis. Party over."

He's on top of me, smiling. Either he thinks this is funny or he thinks I don't mean it. He lowers his head to my neck, and I push him off me. Hard.

Travis sits and brushes sand from his tux, an angry expression on his face. "I knew you were a, a—"

"A what?"

"Tease. C'mon let's go." He holds his hand like he'll help me up, then changes his mind and drops it.

"Travis, listen," I say gently. "I didn't mean to lead you on. It's just that I like someone else, ya know?"

"Haven't you ever heard of friends with benefits?"

I have heard of it and even kinda get it. It's girls like me who feel behind and want to catch up, or who are too curious, or who like a guy but aren't confident enough to make sure he likes her back. Even though I get it and want to be kissed, I'm not willing to compromise.

"I like someone else," I apologize.

"Yeah—Sam. Everyone seems to crush on him. Except he's with Alana. Don't you want to make them a little jealous?"

Sam likes Alana?

"Just take me home." My heart crumbles.

Sand has gotten inside my gown and the grit scratches as I sit on the vinyl seats in Travis's truck. I feel dirty. The over ripe moon fills my window. Earlier I'd imagined it looked romantic, but it's only a cold, remote reflection of light.

# CHAPTER FIFTEEN

Sometimes when my eyelids flutter open and I see the sunlight peeking through my blinds, I forget who I am for a minute. It's like I'm this new person and I don't remember my life. That was today until I remembered Rodeo Bob's, the Snow Ball, the beach with Travis and afterwards with Mom.

The phone rings; I roll over and read the clock—9:30. It's Lexie. I just know it.

"I'll be there in thirty minutes, so be ready," she says.

"I just woke up."

"So, get going."

I'm about to hang up when Lexie says, "Listen, if I bring the black dress, how will you sneak it in?"

"Just bring it. I already got caught."

"What?"

"Yeah. I'll tell you all about it."

After Travis brought me home, he wanted to walk me to the door, which I let him do. Then he wanted to come inside, which I didn't. I don't know what he thought would happen if he came in.

Well, actually I do. He wanted to play kissy face again, but didn't I make my point at the beach? What actually happened was I kissed his cheek, thanked him and ducked inside.

Mom was waiting up for me. "Jane? Where's your dress?"

There was this big silent pause, like someone hit the mute button on the TV.

"That's the other dress you tried, isn't it?" Mom's volume was on, but mine was still off. "Why is there seaweed on your dress?"

Mute.

"Are you going to answer me?"

I'd have liked to but wasn't sure exactly how to say things.

"Where's my necklace? Do you still have that?"

Oh, God. Now that would be the end of my life. I looked down at my chest. Luckily it was there—all tangled with the seashell mermaid necklace. "Yes," I managed.

Mom slumped back in her chair and drew her robe tighter. Her fingernail tapped on the upholstered arm. I hadn't moved from my spot, frozen in the entry hall. "Just go to bed," she said. "We'll discuss this tomorrow."

I slunk off to my room.

"And try not to track sand all over. I mopped today."

So, this is what my day holds. No wonder I lost hope when my memory kicked in.

Rolling out of bed, I step on my pale aqua gown, which lies in a heap totally crusted in seaweed and sand. When I pick it up to hang it, sand sprinkles onto the floor. Ugh—more mess.

As I hang the mermaid gown next to Dolphin Girl at the back of the closet, I reflect on everything that had gone right *and wrong* last night. Going to the Snow Ball with Travis—what was I thinking? Kissing him on the beach—definitely a huge error. The slow dance with Sam was A-okay. And, I still don't think the aqua dress was a mistake. However, not changing back into the black one was a huge one. A mistake, that is.

I shower, spending extra time washing my hair to get the mousse out that's made it feel all stiff. Then I throw on board shorts, a pink tee, and slip into my pink and tan polka dot Vans. After sprinkling a few flakes for Flipper, I head to the kitchen.

Dad sits at the table with the Sports section spread out and a cup of coffee in his hand. When I pour a glass of OJ, he says, "Your Mom left you a list. She's at her book club."

The book club is a bit of a joke, since I've never seen Mom actually read one. It's just an excuse to get together and gossip. But today, I'm glad she's gone all literary. That means our talk is postponed.

"Lexie and I are going Christmas shopping." I take a swig

of juice. "I'll do it later."

"Okay. Have fun."

I wonder for the millionth time if he's mellow or apathetic. Like the way he acted about my costume or even about John's news. Either way, it's a good balance to Mom, because later today we'll have WWIII over my dress. And the list.

A piece of my hair flops down and hits him when I smooch his unshaven cheek.

"Your hair's still wet," he says.

"It'll dry in the Jeep," I explain as the doorbell rings.

Lexie bursts in with the black dress on a hanger. "You're not gonna believe what's on TV! Remember Kelsey Davis?"

Kelsey went to elementary school with us and moved away before middle. She's John's age.

Lexie follows me to my room and grabs the remote while I toss the dress onto the bed. "She's on *Parental Control.*"

Omigod! How mortifying for her. It's almost like something Mom would do—not approve of the guy I'm dating and then set me up on dates with other people. Come to think of it, she probably would've done it to John and Desiree, too.

We stand in front of the TV and a local news broadcast comes on. I grab the remote from her before she can change the channel. "Wait," I say. "Look."

On the screen, there's a reporter with mic in hand. He says, "They've been out there for two days now, and it has some local marine biologists concerned." The camera zooms in to show two dolphins at the edge of the sand bar, circling.

"I saw them last night. That's where we went after the dance."

The screen switches from the dolphins to a headshot of a marine biologist. "It's not their normal habitat and, of course, we're concerned about a possible stranding. If they don't head back out to sea soon, we'll need to lure them there."

They're fine. They spoke to me. I don't know how I know this, but I do.

The news shifts to a traffic accident in Miami. I hand the remote back to Lexie so she can put on MTV. We watch the end of Kelsey's *Parental Control* episode and even though her boyfriend is a real jerk, she stays with him. Duh. Who's gonna date a guy their parents handpicked?

~~~

After shopping, Lexie drops me in the driveway. As I grab bags of Christmas presents from the backseat, I know my liberty from Mom is over.

"So you're coming to Willow's later, right?" she asks.

"It probably depends on how the 'gown discussion' goes."

I gave her all the post-Ball details while we shopped: Travis at the beach, Mom when I got home. After my sad tale, she simply said, "You have the worst luck."

It's not about to improve.

When I walk in, déjà vu. Mom's sitting in the exact same spot as last night, except she's not wearing her bathrobe. Instead, she holds my Fallopian Tubes artwork on her lap. "What's this?" she asks.

She had to go into my room to get that. Typical and oh-so wrong.

"It's some art I did. It's for Lexie's band."

"I can see that. The Fallopian Tubes—right? I heard *all* about it at book club from Mrs. Atwood."

I didn't know Alana's mom was in the book club. Alana! She's behind this.

"She told me this was unveiled for the whole school last night." A fingernail tap. "Don't you think this art and the name of the band is completely inappropriate for young ladies?"

Lexie and I aren't young ladies. But I don't say that. What is Alana trying to do to me? "The name is just funny, Mom. Don't you think the art is a good way of showing fallopian tubes? I didn't know what to draw. It's abstract. It used to be a butterfly."

"I think the name is bad. I think the art is bad. And I think your friend is a bad influence. I think I've known this ever since her piercing and hair cut last year. And I think I should have taken action then. That's what I think."

Action? What is she talking about, action?

"You will not associate with this girl anymore."

*What the—?*

"Am I clear? You will not go places where she will be. She brought you that other dress. I heard all about that too."

"I asked her to bring it. It was my idea, and so was the art."

"Well, maybe your ideas will change with a little less exposure to Lexington Murphy."

No. My ideas won't change. And my friendship with Lexie won't change either. But Alana better watch out.

~~~

"Merry Christmas," I whisper into the phone even though my bedroom door is shut.

"Jane?" Lexie asks.

"Who else?"

Lexie and I have texted every day since Mom forbade me to be friends with her. The first day, when I told Lexie about Mom's new rule, she didn't respond for three whole minutes. I thought maybe she'd been disconnected or didn't get my message or something until *WHAAAAAAAATTTTTTT?!!!!* appeared on my screen, followed by a quick *it figures*.

It cracked me up. Mom might be able to keep me from hanging out with her, but I have no intention of losing my best friend. And today, on Christmas, I miss her so much that I decided to risk a call.

"What'dya get?" I ask.

"These totally bitchin' boots from Mom and Dad and money for the demo fund."

I trace my finger over the wave design on my comforter. "That's awesome! Are you close?"

"It depends on if Willow and Tara got cash. If they did, we might be able to record over break."

I'm so incredibly happy for her and so abysmally sad that I'll miss it.

"How 'bout you?" she asks.

"I got the swim! I still can't believe they gave it to me." I roll over on my bed and look at the poster.

"That's so cool," she says. "How's everything else? Weird?"

Yesterday our text convo was all about how John and Desiree were coming for Christmas and that it would be strange, because the holiday would make it official—our family has changed. They both arrived about an hour ago, right before we opened gifts, and it was surprisingly normal. For me, at least. Mom might feel different.

"She brought the dog. And he lay in the piles of wrapping paper. Desiree stuck a bow on his head. It was adorable." I glance at Flipper like I've betrayed him. "Desiree's really sticking out now. You can't miss that she's preggers."

"How far along is she?"

There's a quick rap on the door. "Jane?" It's Mom.

"Just a sec," I holler.

"You need to pack up the bows." Her voice filters through the door.

"Gotta go," I tell Lexie.

"But how far along?" she wails.

The door swings open as I say, "Almost six months," and flip the phone closed before tucking it under my thigh.

"The bows, Jane." Mom taps her fingernail on my light switch. "I hope that wasn't Lexington."

Geez. It's Christmas, and Mom still won't go back to calling her Lexie.

*Strandings are one of the most disheartening phenomena in the dolphin world. Scientists haven't been able to pinpoint why an animal separates from the pod to go ashore and die. Sometimes it seems they are lost or disoriented. Other times, merely isolated socially. When a dolphin is saved and returned to their family it's a cause for great celebration amongst admirers of this mammal.*
*(Excerpt:* The Magic and Mystery of Dolphins*)*

# CHAPTER SIXTEEN

"The demo last night was unbelievable," Lexie gushes as we stand next to the water fountain before the first bell. "I got my birthday check from Nana and Pops early, so I added it to the Christmas money and then with everyone else's money, we had enough."

"What an awesome birthday present!" I say.

Lexie turns seventeen this coming weekend, and her parents are taking our pod out to dinner. It'll be the first time I haven't celebrated with her in—well—ever since we've been friends. All because Mom won't change her mind.

Today, our return to school from break, is the first time I've actually seen my best friend since we went shopping. Most kids are disappointed to lose the freedom they had over break, but for me it's an improvement, as I gain some by getting out of the house.

It's not like Mom grounded me or anything. But when you can't hang with your best friend and your approved friends hang with her, you might as well be. Grounded, that is. I even missed the first session for The Fallopian Tubes and wish I could have been there because Lexie is so obviously pumped about it.

"Sorry I missed it," I tell her. She takes me through the whole session song by song and then I ask, "Hey, have you seen Sam yet?"

She rolls her eyes when I change the subject. "No sign of him."

The worst part about that whole situation is I haven't seen him since Irwin got sick and I took over as yearbook photographer. He never showed up at the beach. And now I have this huge underground zit on my chin. Not. Too. Attractive.

"How bad is this?" I ask Lexie, pointing at the zit.

"Not too bad," she lies. I love her for it.

The best part about seeing Sam will be lunch. Before the end of last semester, we got our new schedules and our lunch periods were moved to the regular junior time.

"You'll still eat with me?" I asked him.

"Of course," he said without hesitation.

So today will be our debut as lunch buddies before God, the

trophy case and everyone. It won't matter that I didn't fit in at the dance.

My first clue something is wrong is when Lexie grabs my wrist, shakes it and asks, "Have you talked to Sam since the Ball?"

I freeze. "No."

Sam never calls or texts me. We're Facebook friends—whatever that means—and I'm ashamed to admit I've stalked his page. Only Lexie knows this. But, he didn't even post there over the break. I have serious Sam withdrawal.

I follow her eyes to the trophy case. Sam's arm is draped around Alana's waist, his hand on her hip.

Is that a live fish flopping in my stomach?

Travis stares at me, blabbering and acting like a knob. What else is new? Brittney, Ashley and Chase stare too. When Travis points, Sam and Alana look over their shoulders. No smiles, no waves.

Oh God. Will I never be able to fit in with them? Did I just imagine Sam liked me? Maybe I made it up, or made it bigger than it really was. Maybe he was just flirting and it was no big deal.

The image of a dolphin dying alone on a sand bar flashes through my mind. It kills me.

"Why'd I have to go with Travis? Why'd I have to take over for Irwin?" I ask Lexie. "Why couldn't Alana? She's on yearbook too, you know?"

My questions are rhetorical, but she answers anyway, "Because stuff like that never happens to girls like Alana. It's partly why she stopped being our friend."

~~~

"You're okay with Sam sitting with us, right?" I ask Lexie in the café. I consider the roast beef. New Year's is a great time to make changes, but I end up grabbing my usual tuna and place it on the tray. Nothing much at school has changed, except lunch hour.

Sam strolls into the cafeteria. I wave at him. He's looking all around, but not in my direction. When he finally does, his face is blank. Like he doesn't see me. Then he breaks into a smile, sidles up to Alana, and they head to the line together.

I keep thinking Sam's just being friendly to her because that's how he is. I keep expecting him to split off from her and head my way. I keep hoping this right up until he puts his tray at the trophy case table.

Lexie stabs a tater tot and wiggles her fork at me. "He's not worth the heartache."

"He is. You even said we looked like we belong together." Willow plants herself next to me and I tell Lexie, "You just don't know him the way I do."

Willow twists open her juice bottle. "Know who?"

"We're talking about Sam," Lexie says, "and Jane's obsession with him."

"He's gonna eat with us today, right?"

I nudge Willow and point in Sam's direction. Her eyes widen. "Oh. I'm sure it's nothing. Maybe he needs to talk to her for a class or something."

He never showed up at the beach. I wish I shared Willow's optimism, but between the hall and now this, it's not happening. I ignore her comment and glare at Lexie. "I am not obsessed."

"It's all right if you are," Willow says at the same time Lexie says, "You are."

Fine. Everyone thinks I'm obsessed with Sam.

Lucas puts his tray next to Lexie and gives her a little smooch on her cheek.

She makes googly eyes at him, so I guess it's easy for her to be critical of the guy I like. "All I'm saying is, there are other fish in the sea." She's right about this, but not all of them are dolphin boy.

"Who are we talking about?" Lucas takes a big bite of his burger.

"*Sam Rojas.*"

"Oh, wite," Lucas says with a full mouth. He swallows. "Nice guy."

"See," I say to Lexie. "Everyone likes Sam."

"I never said he wasn't a good guy. Everyone does like him, including Alana apparently, so you just need to get over it." Lexie stabs another tater tot. "Look, Jane. The thing is, he's in with that group. There are a lot of other guys in this school who would want to hang out with us."

And there it is—the whole damn pod thing again.

After lunch, my insides are quiet and hollow while I drift from class to class like smoke, vanishing silently. Finally, before English, I see Sam at his locker and become solid again. I walk up behind him and put my hands over his eyes.

"Guess who?" I ask, but Sam's shoulders droop. He doesn't play along. I take my hands away and lean to face him. "Hey! How was your Christmas?"

"Good." Sam is stony-faced, concentrating all his attention on the book swap.

"What'd Santa bring?"

Without looking at me, he says, "I got the new iPod."

"That's cool."

There's this awkward pause while Sam stares into his locker, transfixed by his Biology text. I wish for the bazillionth time we'd never stopped to see Alana's car. Or that Irwin had a stronger stomach.

When Sam doesn't speak, I do. "Mine was good, thanks for asking. I didn't get any coal this year."

Sam smiles. It's brittle. And he doesn't ask what I got, so I volunteer. "My parents gave me the dolphin swim in the Keys. I get to go over Spring Break."

This brings on a fleeting smile from Sam, and then his face turns angry again. "That's not all you got, right?"

I've been foggy all day, and this remark certainly doesn't clear up anything.

"Jungle gym kisses. You're an animal, I hear," Sam continues.

I snort a laugh and expect Sam to laugh along with me. "You mean Travis?"

"You went to the beach after the dance, right?" Sam's staring at me and he's angry.

"Yeah." Where this is going makes me queasy. "But you didn't."

Sam shoves his text into his backpack. "I did. And I saw you. On the beach. With Travis. You guys decided to cut out early, huh?" Sam slams his locker, spins the dial and walks away.

I hurry to catch him. "What does that mean?"

"You know what it means. You were there."

I grab Sam by the arm and make him stop. "Listen, I kept looking for you, but you weren't there."

"Alana ran out of gas. I had to walk to get it for her and when we finally made it to the beach, you were sprawled out with my best friend."

"Listen, Sam," I plead, "you don't understand. We only

kissed a couple of times, but he tasted like Rodeo Bob's, so I asked him to take me home. Nothing happened."

"Nothing? That's not what I heard."

"That's the truth. What did Travis say?"

Sam and I stand in the middle of the hall, creating a traffic jam, and other kids on their way to class have to loop around us.

He pulls his arm away and jerks it twice before stalking off.

*Whaa—?* It takes a minute for it to sink in. *Omigod.* He thinks I hooked up with Travis.

Travis. What a d-bag! I can't believe he told Sam we hooked up. Why would he do that? What was I thinking when I kissed him? Why did I even go to the ball with him? I can't believe Sam believes him instead of me.

A weird thought pops into my head. All day today I thought everyone was looking at me because of my dress, or the way I danced or because I helped Irwin, but what if all the talk was about me and Travis?

~~~

When the final bell rings, I'm ready to be out of here. English and Bio totally sucked. Clavell lectured about the role of fungi in our world, which should have brought a comment from Sam. But he sat with Travis and kept his eyes trained on the lab table, like I was a parasitic fungi—athlete's foot or something.

I wish I didn't have yearbook after school and could go straight home. Or, better yet, to the preserve. No such luck.

As I walk by the trophy case in the main hall, Travis, Chase and Ashley are hanging out. Sam's there too, his arm slung over Alana's shoulder. Travis points, laughs, makes his hands into a shark fin and sings the theme from Jaws. "Do, do...do, do, dodododo."

Everyone cracks up.

I flush hot. My hands clench, and my fingernails dig into my palms. "You're disgusting and a liar," I yell and stomp off.

I don't know what Travis is doing now, but can hear Alana's shrill squeal pierce the air. My skin is blistering, I'm so pissed. A hot tear dribbles down my cheek.

By the time I reach the Journalism lab, I can't hear her anymore. The light is on over the darkroom, so hiding there is out of the question. Inside the cubby labeled with my name, there's a stack of photos from the Snow Ball. A note from Mr. Fischer is attached with one of Irwin's clothes pins:

*Jane,*
*Thought you might like to try your hand at a spread. If you have any questions, find me or ask Alana for help.*

*Mr. Fischer*

Fat chance. Asking Alana, that is. I don't care if she is the editor of the Events section. I can figure this out on my own.

I prop each photo in front of me and then flip it face-down into a pile while my eyes continue to leak. I can't seem to get the whole crying thing under control, and that pisses me off even more. *Just focus on the pictures.*

There are some good ones of Lexie performing. Irwin must not have been wasted yet. Eventually, I come to the shot when Sam pulled me against him. How did I get from there—where I was so close—to him laughing while Travis sang the Jaws theme?

I sense someone standing behind me. Alana hovers over my shoulder. "Mr. Fischer told me he was going to assign this spread to you. You should use that as your dominant photo." She points to the group pic then picks up the stack of photos I'd already flipped through and fans them out like she's playing cards. From the middle she plucks one and lays it on the desk. It's a vertical shot of her dancing with Sam.

The picture opens a hole in my heart.

"This will work on the opposing page. Template three would work best."

After she leaves, I pull up Template 3 on the computer and flip through the stack again. Which of these photos will work to fill smaller holes?

But something inside me revolts. That's. It.

Jealousy washes over me. Dolphins get jealous too, ya know? I read about this female dolphin that attacked Susan

Sarandon while she swam with the girl dolphin's hubby or boyfriend or partner or whatever it is that dolphins have.

And I am jealous of Alana.

First, she got the VW Beetle, my favorite car. Okay, so this one is dumb, I know, but whatever—it still makes me jealous. Second, she got my date for the Snow Ball. Third, she opened her big, *big* mouth—telling her mom about the band and my art. This is nothing new; she had a big mouth when we were friends. But her blab made it so I can't hang with my best friend outside of school. And finally, not only did she get the date, but now it looks like she got Sam.

I'm not going to let her have what she wants on this spread. I refuse to play along, acting all submissive.

Clicking through the templates, I come across one that features two dominant vertical spots—one on each page. I take the group shot and one of the Tubes and head to the darkroom.

*Bang!* Irwin's agitating film.

"Hey!" I yell through the door, "when you're done with that, can you help me to crop some photos?"

~~~

Irwin slowly pushes his glasses up the bridge of his nose after marking up the photos for the Snow Ball spread. He reminds me of an elderly tortoise. I learn how to crop quickly, before his lengthy explanation, but I've come to realize he's methodical about everything and you just have to go with that.

"Thanks, Irwin. Hey! I've been meaning to ask you, how did things go after you got home from the Ball? John said he made sure you got inside okay."

"Yeah. Thanks for calling him. Your sister-in-law was really nice."

"Listen, tomorrow morning—why don't you come and hang out with me at the water fountain? I'll introduce you to Lexie and Willow and Tara—"

"I like to come here." Irwin fiddles with a film case.

"But you don't have any friends."

Two things happen simultaneously. Irwin's face falls, and I realize what I said. *Stupid, stupid, stupid.*

"I didn't mean—"

"I know what you meant." Irwin's face reverts to the bitter expression he wore the first day I met him.

# CHAPTER SEVENTEEN

Pregnant women are everywhere.

I never noticed them at the mall or the grocery store or the movies until Desiree got pregnant. They walk around with the world's future stored in their bellies, mostly unnoticed by the rest of us.

Today I'm surrounded by tomorrow. In the waiting room at the OB-GYN, it's the biggest number of pregnant women I've ever seen in one place at one time. Flat-stomached, I'm out of place.

When Desiree asked me to come along for her monthly check-up, I was surprised because it seems so private. But she said, "You're going to be the baby's auntie," and "I think you'll find it enlightening." How could I pass that up? Especially since I can't hang with Lexie and friends.

"How're you today, missy?" a round nurse dressed in purple asks Desiree after she calls us from the waiting room. She seems to know Desiree and leads her to the scale. The nurse slides the gadget, tapping it gently into place, and records Desiree's weight on her chart. Then she hands her a plastic cup.

"Be right back." Desiree winks at me and disappears into the bathroom.

Our next stop is a chair where Desiree gets her blood pressure taken and her finger stuck. Earlier this year in Bio, we had to type our blood. I nearly fainted and can't watch now.

After this, we're on the move again. This time it's the examining room. The nurse hands Desiree a flimsy paper gown and closes the door behind her.

Through the door I hear her cheerful voice, fading as she walks away: "How're you today, missy?" I guess she says this to everyone.

I scope out the walls while Desiree undresses. They're decorated with the same corny posters that hung in the waiting room: a woman looking ecstatic while riding her bike, a woman looking ecstatic while flying a kite. In the waiting room they had a woman looking ecstatic while walking by the ocean. At least I understood her happiness—she's close to dolphins, but all the photos remind me of a Kotex ad.

Desiree situates herself on the table and folds her hands over her belly.

I point at the wall art and make a face.

"Yeah, they could update those." She wiggles and swings her legs back and forth, trying to get comfortable.

"Do you have to get your finger stuck every time?" I ask.

"Yup."

This news—more than any sex ed class—is enough to ensure I'll use contraception if I ever start doing it. No way do I want to get pregnant. I hate finger sticks. Cripes, getting the tattoo really hurt, but at least at the end I had something pretty to show for it.

It's quiet in the exam room. There's no ticking clock, but time stretches in mind-bending ways until Desiree says, "John and I would like you to be the godmother."

"Really?" I ask, not knowing what that meant. It seems like there should be someone else she'd want. "Can I ask you something?"

"Sure."

"What happened with your family? Why don't you see them?"

Desiree's eyes meet mine. "Oh, that. Well, my dad was in the military. He was very big on rules."

Like Mom. "And, you didn't stay in the lines?"

"It was okay when I was little, but when I hit thirteen I got rebellious."

"Like me."

Desiree gave me a strange look. "You're not the least bit rebellious. Anyway, we got on each other's nerves and then they wouldn't let me see my boyfriend, so when I turned eighteen I moved away. Far away. That's it. End of story."

"You never saw them again?"

Desiree's eyes get watery. "I think they were relieved when I moved. They never came after me." Her lips tighten.

I fidget on the uncomfortable, backless stool. "Do you think you did the right thing? Leaving?" This question nags me because her situation seems to parallel mine.

Desiree picks at invisible lint on her paper gown, so at first I don't think she's going to answer. She sighs. "Life isn't a DVD that you can flip back to an earlier scene you want to replay. If I hadn't left—" she turns to look me in the eyes— "I might not have met John, and he's the best thing in my life."

There's a quick rap at the door, and in walks the nurse midwife. She hurries to a table and scans Desiree's chart, then jots a few notes. Plucking one, two gloves from a box, she's got them on by the time she reaches the examining table. "Everything's good? How are you feeling?"

"Great," Desiree answers.

"You work, right? What do you do?"

"Restaurant."

"On your feet," the midwife says while writing and then lifts one of Desiree's feet. Her ankles are swollen. "You've got a little edema," she notes. "We need to keep an eye on it."

"I'll be fine."

"Well, we'll keep an eye anyway." She's moves to Desiree's mid-section, opens her gown and handles her belly like she's buying a melon. I expect her to knock on it any minute now.

"Okay. Let's have a look at her," the midwife says. She takes some Vaseline-looking gloop and rubs it on a piece of equipment that reminds me of the thingy they use to restart your heart on TV shows. She rubs a little more of the greasy stuff on Desiree's bare belly and points to the screen. "There she is."

In front of me, an image appears. I can't make anything out.

"See—" the midwife points— "here's her thigh."

I squint my eyes. I guess I can kinda see it. There's a sudden movement on the screen, and Desiree touches her belly.

"She flipped over," the midwife comments. "She's mooning us. Now you can tell she's a girl."

I laugh and stare at the blob on the screen. It's not clear to me. "How?"

"Well we're never a hundred percent sure, but if she was a boy we'd see another appendage right about here." She uses her pen to point.

A niece. That's nice. "Have you picked a name?" I ask.

"John and I picked the name Lily for a girl."

The midwife moves the paddle around Desiree's belly in circular motions. "What a nice name."

"I don't know if Mom will like it." I'm thinking out loud—never a good thing.

Desiree looks me straight in the eye. "I don't care. I do."

My heart cartwheels. I wish I could be defiant with Mom, but of course my mom is not Desiree's mom.

"You're Desiree's sister?" The midwife wipes the goo off Desiree's belly.

"Her sister-in-law."

The midwife places her hand behind Desiree's back and props her to a sitting position. Desiree arranges the paper gown around her like we're at fancy restaurant. "And I hope she'll agree to be the godmother."

Tears flood my eyes. I don't know why she picked me.

"Ah, godmothers are important," the midwife says. She rummages through a cupboard and locates a plastic model of a baby. "This is how big the baby is right now," she says and hands me the odd little doll. It's much longer than I thought, but scrawny and light as a feather. When the baby is curled, it barely extends past the palm of my hand.

I hand the model back. "Her belly's a lot bigger than this."

"That's because the baby is surrounded by amniotic fluid. It's a cushion for protection." She points to a picture on the wall.

I'd forgotten about the fluid, even though they taught us about it in sex ed. It's amazing; almost as if we all start life as dolphins. "Is it salt water?" I ask.

The midwife laughs. "Well, there's electrolytes in it containing some salt, protein, carbohydrates, even the baby's urine."

Yuck. Maybe not exactly like the ocean. Or on second thought...

She lays the model of the baby on the table next to Desiree. "Okay. I'll see you in four weeks." She pauses. "What's your due date again?"

"March fourteenth," Desiree says.

The nurse-midwife pulls a wheel from her pocket and spins it. "Right. Four weeks is fine, but I want you to keep an eye on those ankles and if anything changes, come in sooner."

March 14th is before Spring Break and my dolphin swim. Up to this point, the baby has only been an idea for me, but now I realize Lily will be here soon. Amazing.

*Out of water, dolphins become overheated very quickly.*
*Their skin can actually burn, leaving scars.*
*(Excerpt:* The Magic and Mystery of Dolphins*)*

# CHAPTER EIGHTEEN

English class has always been one of my favorites, even if Breckenridge does have a few strange quirks. He rolls his tie up to the knot, holds it in place and lets it unfurl for emphasis. "Does anyone know what today is?"

There are quips around the room that range from "Monday" to "Your birthday?" to "February second."

Breckenridge paces at the front of the room and plays with his tie again.

Should I put his necktie on the mobile?

As he lets go of it, he says, "Well, you're right about almost everything, except it's not my birthday." He laughs at himself. "February in Florida has the most glorious weather. Too bad it's the shortest month of the year. But I have to tell you, when I lived in Pennsylvania and was buried under snow and ice, it felt like the longest."

January had been the longest month for me. The days just blurred together—no Sam, lots of work for yearbook, missing Lexie except for lunches. The only thing that was interesting was going to the doctor with Desiree.

He stops pacing, leans against the corner of his desk. Roll. "One thing makes February bearable—smack in the middle of the month—we've got Valentine's Day. Love makes everything better." Unwind.

It's great my teacher is a romantic, but I'm not sure he's right. It hurts to look one row over and two desks up at Sam's profile.

Breckenridge walks behind his desk and picks up a handful of paperback books. "So, with love in the air, it's only fitting to study Shakespeare's *Romeo and Juliet.*"

A few groans.

"Oh Romeo, Romeo where for art thou, Romeo," Steven says in a falsetto.

Breckenridge laughs. "Good, Steven. You've already memorized a line, but there's a lot more than that to the story." He walks each row, placing books on the desks. "This is one of the saddest love stories of all time. Please read all of Act One by Tuesday." The groans increase, but Breckenridge ignores them.

"By the end of this play, some of you will hope you never read Shakespeare again." He stops at my desk, places the book and smiles at me. "But there will be others who will enjoy this so much, they'll enroll in my AP Shakespeare course next year." He moves through the rest of the rows silently as I flip through the book.

Pulling the TV cart to the front of the room, he continues, "Today we'll watch *West Side Story*, which is a modern retelling of the tale."

When the movie comes on, Steven fakes a cough. "Modern?"

The class laughs.

The movie's old, but by the time we reach the scene where they sing "America," everyone is into it. Plus, Steven keeps calling everyone Daddy-O and even Breckenridge thinks it's funny.

Right before the bell, Breckenridge stops the movie before it's finished and says we'll watch the end on Monday. "As you read *Romeo and Juliet* this weekend, think about how it compares to *West Side Story*. Both are stories of forbidden love. Be prepared to discuss this."

I look at the frozen scene where Maria gazes at Tony from the fire escape. It's clear how much she loves him, how hopeful she is. I wish I shared her hope, but I'm not convinced I want to watch the end of this movie. After all, Breckenridge said it was one of the saddest love stories of all time.

~~~

I'm sorting photos for winter sports into three piles: *Yes*, *Probably*, and *Maybe*. The trashcan sits by my feet for the *No*s. The yearbook lab is a flurry of activity before school because we're on top of a deadline for more than seventy-five pages.

Alana marches up to me, holding a proof of the Snow Ball spread. "I can't believe you did this!" She points to the close-up of Sam and me in the dominant spot. "He wasn't your date."

She's pissed, and there's a part of me that couldn't care less. "He would have been if you hadn't pulled the parking lot scam."

Alana's mouth drops open. Actually, I don't know for sure that Sam was going to ask me, but he might have. And if so, we might be a couple now instead of…of…crap, I don't even know what we are. Ex-lunch/word-game buddies?

"You're living in a dream world, Jane," Alana says in a snotty tone. "He'd never date a trashy tramp-stamp girl. Unless it was for one thing."

Someone says, "Ooh, you shouldn't let her talk to you like that, girl."

A part of me knows that's right. I should stand up for myself. But another part wonders, *Is she right? I'm not good enough for Sam?* And still another part realizes once and for all that this friendship is done.

I toss a blurry volleyball photo I took into the trash and eye her. "Don't be so sure, Alana." My voice is shaky. It's not the kind of comeback I'd like to shoot at her, but it makes her freeze for a second and that's enough.

~~~

When you start your day all flustered, you need your first class to bring tranquility. Mine doesn't. Mrs. Fonseca distributes last week's Algebra test and the top of mine has a red, circled 63 staring at me like some kind of bizarre eyeball.

My heart sinks. I knew I didn't do well, but never thought my grade would drop this low. The problem, *my* problem, stems from my inability to grasp the quadratic formula. Sometimes, when Mrs. Fonseca is teaching, I feel like I'm sitting in a classroom in another country—that's how foreign this equation is to me.

I hate, absolutely hate getting a D. But what makes it worse is knowing there'll only be a couple more tests in this grading period. My math skills in averages and probabilities are decent, so I know it's improbable I'll be able to average a B.

There's a note next to the D: *Please see me after class.* I rub my forehead with my left hand. This is bad.

When the bell rings, everyone starts filing out and Mrs.

Fonseca says, "Jane?"

Now I rub my forehead with both hands. Unzipping my book bag, I put in the math text, then my homework spiral, then my pencil, and finally the test. I zip it while all the other kids file past Mrs. Fonseca's desk, dropping their papers one by one into her basket. I wait until everyone is out of the room before I walk up.

She looks at me across her desk, over the top of her glasses. "Jane, you seem to be struggling with this unit. Is there a problem?"

Yeah. The quadratic formula isn't my thing. "The equation, I mean the formula... I don't know." I shift my backpack from one shoulder to the other.

"The quadratic formula is like every other equation, so I don't understand why you're struggling. You've always been a 'B' student before, but if you need extra practice, I can tutor you before school."

My shoulders sag and the backpack slips off. "I can't before school. I'm on yearbook and we have a big deadline. I have to be there every day."

"Do you have another resource?"

Resource? I think she means, do I know a person who gets this. John? Brendon/Brandon? Maybe Lucas. Definitely not Lexie.

"I can ask around," I say.

"Well, you need to. We have quiz on Monday and interims go home on Tuesday. If I don't see improvement, I'll request a conference with your parents."

Great, three days. Can I learn it in that time?

~~~

On Wednesday, we watch the end of *West Side Story* and I struggle not to cry in class when Maria says, "*Te adoro*, Tony," while he lies dead in the middle of the playground.

It hits me, just as surely as if I'd been in the gang fight between the Jets and the Sharks—some couples are impossible. They aren't supposed to be. Like John and Desiree because of their age difference. Like someone from the trophy case with someone from the water fountain. It's a big no-go. According to the rules of love, Sam is supposed to be with Alana.

"Now for oral presentations." Breckenridge interrupts my revelation. He pairs boys with girls and gives each pair a scene.

"Steven and Becca, you'll read the balcony scene. Steven, I know you'll nail this one—you already have the 'Romeo, Romeo where for art thou Romeo' part down."

Steven stands, takes a pretend bow, and everyone laughs. Breckenridge keeps assigning scenes until I think he's done. I breathe a sigh of relief at remaining unscathed.

"Hmm…" He rolls his tie, and it's mesmerizing. "I need

one more pair for the scene after they spend the night together."

"That's the scene I want," Steven says, and everyone laughs.

"Omigod! They spend the night together?" Becca asks.

"I know. Pretty racy for four hundred years ago." Breckenridge grins. "That should ensure you keep reading."

Because I read ahead, I know the scene. It's their promise to each other.

"Ah. Got it." Breckenridge's tie unfurls. "Sam, you'll be Romeo to Jane's Juliet. And everyone, please read through Act Two by Wednesday."

No! He can't pair us. Rehearsing the scene with Sam will be impossible. He's only just started to acknowledge me again with a wave in the cafe or a *hey* in the main hall.

One row over and two desks up, Sam turns in his seat to look at me, resting his tongue on that chipped tooth and thinking God knows what. Then he nods, smiles and pats his copy of *Romeo and Juliet*.

Like the English dork that I am, I read all the explanatory notes at the end of the book, including Shakespeare's use of fate.

Well. This feels like fate is intervening; but is it going to help or hurt me?

# CHAPTER NINETEEN

Mom props two crib sets next to each other on a dresser in Aisle 7 of Babies R Us. "Which one?" One comforter is mostly pink with white; the other is mostly white with pink.

My favorite is a brightly colored tropical fish design Mom vetoed because "it's not for a baby girl." I think Desiree may have liked the tropical fish better too, but she couldn't shop with us because her ankles were super swollen this morning and Mom decided she needed to stay off her feet.

"I guess that one." I point to the mostly pink comforter.

"I think I'll buy both, let Desiree pick, and we'll return the other." Mom places the crib sets into our already overflowing shopping cart.

I had no idea how many things you needed for babies. We've got blankets, binkies, booties and bottles; diapers, diaper pail, diaper bag, diaper cream, and wipes; onesies, gowns with elastic bottoms, T-shirts, and clothes in newborn, 3- and 6-month sizes.

I hold up the clothes and it's hard to tell which is which because there is hardly any difference. "Why so many sizes?"

"Oh honey, they grow so fast," Mom says.

But I think she may have gone overboard because the baby can't wear the six-month size for, well, six months. Desiree will get to the store before then.

"Are we done?" I ask.

"Not even close." Mom holds a registry form. It's not Desiree's picks, since she never registered. But Mom asked for a blank one to have a complete list. "We've got to pick the big items. Crib, changing table, stroller, car seat, swing. Babies need a lot of stuff, Jane."

Mom's totally in her element. This is what she lives for, and it drives me crazy. And this is what my weekends have been reduced to without a best friend. Or a boyfriend, since Sam and Alana have cultivated their couplehood.

I'm so not into this.

"Where are the strollers?" Mom asks no one in particular and turns the cart in circles, reading the overhead signs. Aisle 3. She points the cart, and I follow.

On the way to strollers, Mom gets sidetracked by a special display with sentimental items like baby books and kits to make footprints out of clay. The display features christening gowns and she examines the white, lacy dresses, taking one off the hanger, flipping it inside out, inspecting the seams and holding it to the light like some kind of rare stamp. The whole ritual embarrasses me.

She scowls at the price tag. "I wonder if Desiree is planning on having the baby christened? I'm sure I still have the gown you wore, and it's much nicer than any of these."

"I think so. She asked me to be the godmother."

Mom, who has been irritatingly chipper all day, shuts down. Her hand freezes on the way to re-hanging the gown.

"A couple weeks ago—on the way to her appointment," I add, filling the emptiness.

"You can't be the godmother." Mom re-hangs the gown without looking at me.

"Why not?"

"It's too much responsibility for a sixteen-year-old. It's nice Desiree thought of you, but she should have asked me first. She's not thinking clearly about this. Don't worry. I'll talk to her."

I don't know if Mom means Desiree should have asked her to be the godmother or asked for her *opinion* on choosing me. Whichever one it is, I'm not worried. Pissed? Yeah, well, I was kinda excited to be a godmother.

And either way, Desiree won't be happy when Mom sticks her nose in.

Mom steers the cart to the stroller aisle. "I'm not really

surprised she didn't think this through. The baby's due in about a month, and she hadn't bought anything yet." I can't tell if she's talking to me or to herself.

"I thought you were starting to like her."

"I do like her. But that doesn't mean I want you to be like her. Or that I want your life to be like hers."

"You don't get it," I say.

Mom takes a stroller off the shelf for inspection. "Oh, I get it, all right. Desiree's a twenty-nine-year-old pregnant waitress who's married to your brother. She has no degree but takes classes every once and a while. She has virtually no savings, no house, no financial stability." Mom's face reddens, and her voice is as loud as it ever gets. She's trying to unlock the stroller, to see how it opens, but it's stuck.

"All those things—those things you worry about are so, so—superficial," I yell. "Money, money, money. That's all you ever think about. I'm sure if her parents helped she'd have a degree." My fists clench at my sides.

"Well, I'm not sure she would. She's got no direction. But that isn't even the point. The point is, her parents didn't help her because she cut off ties with them." She taps her fingernail on the stroller, a signal for me to stop. Mom lowers her voice, but other shoppers have noticed we're having a disagreement, because a couple people came to look at strollers and turned around instantly, leaving Aisle 3 to us alone.

"You have no idea why she left her family behind at eighteen, do you? Well, I'll tell you why. They were like you."

"Like me? What do you mean?"

"Too many damn rules!"

"Watch your language, young lady," Mom commands. "That's not true."

"It *is* true. She told me. And you know what else she told me? Her parents wouldn't let her see her boyfriend. It's what you did with Lexie."

"I'm pretty sure I made the right decision with that one." *Tap, tap.* "She's never had any manners."

"Screw manners," I yell, and wave my arms, hitting a teddy bear. He falls to the ground. I can't believe I'm yelling at my Mom in the middle of a store. I've never even yelled at her at home.

"Jane, you need to calm down. This is not the place or the time." Mom picks up the teddy, starts to put it on the shelf, but adds it to the cart. She steers the cart away from Aisle 3, with me close on her heels.

"I'm sick of your manners and rules. You don't even follow them. What etiquette book told you it would be okay to buy all this," I wave my hand above the overloaded cart, "without even asking Desiree what she wants?"

This stuns Mom. She stops pushing the cart, and her fingernail hovers. She lowers her voice. "I thought it was important for the baby to have a proper start. I'm going to be the grandparent, after all."

"All you think about is yourself. What about Desiree's feelings? You think of her as a kid, but she's not. She's going to be a mom. You need to think of her as a parent." I wonder why it's easier for me to fight for Desiree than it is to fight for myself.

Mom's response is level and cool. "Parents set boundaries, Jane. I worry about Desiree being able to do this. I worry about John—he's so young."

Every muscle in my body tenses. "Your boundary is a barbed-wire fence. You try to keep everything perfectly ordered. You don't allow any mistakes."

Mom stares at the floor. "That's not true," she says barely audible, playing with one of the binkies.

"You need to wake up, or I'll do what Desiree did when she turned eighteen. I swear, I'll leave and never come back." Now I'm fighting for myself.

"I hope not," Mom steers the cart to the register. Her hands shake as she places clothes, diapers and other paraphernalia on the counter.

Good. Finally I got to her.

Then she smiles at the cashier. "Hi, how're you today?" Like everything is just peachy, like we're not having the biggest fight of our life. What a phony! Mom continues to unload the cart. "You've still got a bit of growing up to do."

Her dismissal scorches me. "Yeah. If you'd let me."

I've always wanted her approval, but it seems out of reach. I'm about ready to say, screw approval.

~~~

Tuesday after dinner, I finally work up the courage to hand Mom my interim report. Her eyes dart from my grades to teacher comments, including the requested conference with Mrs. Fonseca.

I bombed the quiz on Monday. My interim shows a C. Barely.

"A seventy in Algebra? That's not good. Why does Mrs. Fonseca want to talk to me?"

"I— My grade is getting worse. It might go down. I mean, it will go down. I don't get the quadratic formula."

"Well, that's unacceptable."

I knew this would be her reaction, but don't know how she thinks I can fix it. "Look, I didn't try to get a C." I neglect to mention the Ds and Fs I've gotten lately.

Mom taps her finger on the table. "I refuse to go through this again." What is she talking about? "First your brother, and now you. He got into UF and then walked away. You won't even get in with grades like that." She taps the fingernail with a steady *tick, tick.* "What's happening to this family? What's next with you?"

What does John have to do with the quadratic formula?

Mom smooths the interim flat on the table with her palms, ironing out my wrinkles. "You know how important grades are to me. Everything else is a privilege."

I don't even know what everything else refers to. She's taken Lexie away, and I lost Sam. Yearbook? Is that what she means? Fine. "So you want me to give up yearbook?"

Mom glances at the ceiling like an answer is printed there. Then, her fingernail becomes a machine gun staccato. "Yes, no more yearbook. And the dolphin swim is postponed until you get this Algebra grade fixed."

What? That was my Christmas present! I can't believe that's my punishment. "Don't take away the dolphins. Can't I just be grounded again for a month?"

Mom shakes her head.

"Two months?"

"The dolphin swim is postponed," Mom says with one final tap.

"That sucks," I say under my breath and glare at her. She thinks my grade is unacceptable. How would she feel if I gave her a grade as my mother and she failed?

Because she would. Right now I would give her a big, fat F for epic fail.

Living in this house is unacceptable.

My life is unacceptable.

She's wrong about me, and she's wrong about this punishment or privilege or whatever she wants to call it. And you know what else? Desiree was wrong, too.

I *am* a rebel.

# CHAPTER TWENTY

I pop up—wide awake—and look at the clock. It's 3:30 a.m. Immediately, I begin replaying my disagreement with Mom. I fell asleep thinking about bad grades, no dolphin swim, no social life—all of it. As soon as I wake, the thoughts loop some more.

I don't know how to fight back.

It seems like running away is my only option to be free. But the thought of leaving scares me. So I crawl out of bed and turn on my desk lamp. Sam's face peers at me from the corkboard. "What should I do?" I ask the drawing.

Sitting at the desk, I pull a piece of paper from my sketchbook, but I'm so angry I can't think of a thing to draw. So instead I scribble a list of everything that's wrong with my life. When I reach item #10, I realize the list is something Mom would do.

She's turned me into her.

I haul my duffle off the top shelf of my closet. Toss in some necessities: underwear, board shorts, T-shirts, flip flops, my can't-live-without jean shorts and one hoodie. My favorite book—*The Magic and Mystery of Dolphins*. Photography stuff. What else?

Hands on my hips, I look around the room. Dolphin Girl? It's ridiculous. I won't need a Halloween costume, but I can't bear to leave it behind. Right before I zipper it, I pluck Sam's picture from the corkboard and also decide to bring the list I started this morning, in case I ever need a reminder about why I did this.

What time is it now? 4:12. That didn't take long.

I can't leave until after Mom and Dad have gone to work, so I need to find another way to kill time. Going back to sleep is not an option.

Staring at my dolphin poster, I zone out. It's almost like sleepwalking as I glide over to it and tug on the upper right corner. The poster catches and tears in a diagonal gash. The rip is huge, at least a third of the poster. No turning back now. I take down the rest and pitch it into a pile.

The anger from earlier is gone. My insides feel empty. I grab soft lead pencils from my desk and outline the scene I'm going to create. A pod of dolphins swimming above a beautiful, colorful coral reef. I fill the wall across from my bed.

When the sketch is complete, I pull large, labeled

Rubbermaid storage containers from under my bed. Art supply organization, courtesy of Mom. I shove the ones containing acrylic paints and brushes along the far wall next to the mangled poster.

Now, where is my palette?

I stick my head under the bed skirt, see it along the far side and pull it out. Dust bunnies cling to it. I can hear Mom's *you should take better care of your things*. It pisses me off that she's right.

Taking my favorite large brush, I paint in big, sweeping strokes the first layer of the ocean, leaving space around the areas where I'll include the dolphin pod and coral reef. I'm underwater now, the paintbrush is my snorkel.

Working faster than I usually do, the paint flows onto the walls in exactly the right places. Ordinarily I fiddle and re-do and re-do, but I'm satisfied with the art that's emerging. At least for now.

The smell of coffee breaks my trance. I hear my parents' morning ritual: the shower running in Mom's bath. Dad's footsteps on the stairs.

What time is it? 7:27.

I tuck the paintbrush behind my ear, locking the door before someone comes.

"What's that smell? Are you painting in there?" Mom asks.

"Working on my mobile." My voice has a slight quiver in it.

"Okay, but you should stop soon to get ready for school.

See you later, honey."

Much later.

After I do sneaky things, like getting tattooed or switching out my gown, I suffer. This morning is no different as I watch Mom's car pull out of the driveway. Guilt. I'll be running away and skipping. But I don't see another solution. Five minutes later, Dad leaves.

I re-open my door to air the room.

My hair's fallen into my face. While holding the paintbrush, I use the back of my hand to push it out of my eyes.

The mural surprises me as I consider what to paint next. Light filters through the aqua to indigo water. The reef is scarlet and flame and wine, all textured. I'll paint Flipper into the picture. Even though he's a freshwater fish, it's the closest thing to freedom I can give him.

A pod of dolphins is situated above the reef. Creating the look of movement is so difficult, but somehow I've pulled off the sensation they're swimming.

I want to paint myself with the dolphins, except I can't. Not yet.

My stomach grumbles and I glance at the clock. 9:15. It doesn't seem possible I've been doing this for five hours straight. I glance at the duffle, my paintbrush, the mural, and decide it's time to go.

~~~

The sun is low in the sky when footsteps from behind distract me from the sketch I'm working on—a self-portrait in four stages where I start as plain Jane and by the fourth picture I'm a dolphin. I turn to see who's there. It's the preserve's ranger. The guy who hardly ever steps out of his trailer. "Miss, I'm afraid you'll have to leave."

Before I left the house this morning, I removed Mom's list from the fridge, crammed it into the duffle and replaced it with a note held up by the Do Not Ignore magnet: *Taking away the dolphin swim was wrong.*

That's it. The note, and the nearly finished mural in my room. That should send a clear message about what I think of her rules.

I didn't know where I was going, but my feet carried me to the preserve. All day, I've wished and wondered if I could live here somehow. It's a dumb idea—no tent, no supplies, but that doesn't stop me from thinking about it.

The day had been peaceful and solitary until ranger man showed up. "I need to close the park," he says, glancing at the large duffle I'm leaning against, then rubs his hand over a yin-yang tattoo on his forearm.

Cool design, but I like my dolphin better.

Nodding, I unzip the huge bag and pack the sketch pad,

drawing tools and what's left of my bag of Sun Chips. "See ya!" I wave, and weave my way back across the raised walkways.

When I reach the entrance, he slides the chain link gate closed and pad locks it.

I need a place to go. On my cell there are two new messages—both from Mom. Yeah, right. Like I'm gonna call her.

Speed-dial John. He answers after one ring. "Hey! Janey-bo-baney, what's new?"

I figure it makes no sense to make small talk. "I ran away. Can you come get me?"

Ten minutes later, the ancient Camry pulls onto the shoulder alongside the gate. He pops the trunk, and I heave the duffle and backpack into it.

"I'm still working, so you have to come to the restaurant with me," he says as I duck into the passenger seat.

Fine with me. I have no curfew now.

~~~

The restaurant isn't very busy—only three of the fifteen tables are taken. Diners eat at two of them, and Desiree sits at one in the corner with her feet propped up on a plastic milk crate.

I drop my duffle next to the crate and plop into a chair across from her. She's filling shakers with sea salt from a huge carton and gourmet peppercorns from a jug.

"Need help?" I ask.

"Sure." Desiree slides a cluster of pepper shakers to me, like a dealer doling out chips in a casino.

The atmosphere here is so comfortable. Warm, spicy smells waft from the kitchen and the decorations are funky and eclectic. It hits me that John has worked here for almost nine months and I've only been once before, two weeks after John started back in May.

When we walked in, Mom had said, "Interesting décor."

But although she didn't approve, I thought it was cool the way none of the tables, chairs, plates or silverware matched. Sconces in every style from art deco to colonial lined the walls, casting a cozy indirect light. When John came to take our order, he put a plate of homemade hummus and crispy pita chips in the middle of the table. Mom made the same face she'd made when looking at the menu. "Is there any way I can get a plain turkey sandwich? With a slice of tomato?"

"Of course," John said. "But you ought to try the cucumber sauce, it's great."

"I'll stick with plain."

Not too surprising if you think about what she named her kids.

Mom dotted a little hummus on the end of her tongue and shook her head. Dad and I didn't mind; more for us. We scarfed it down. Then the sandwich came. Turkey piled high on thick-sliced bread with sunflower seeds embedded in it. It was easy to tell Mom wasn't keen on the bread. She opened the sandwich and, horror, they'd put on cucumber sauce. She waved John over and showed him.

"Do you want a new sandwich?"

"No. I'll just wipe the sauce off." She used her napkin to get most of it while John hovered at our table.

We never went back after that, which was probably fine with John.

"The hummus here is awesome," I say to Desiree.

"Yeah. It is." She gets up and shuffles to the kitchen, ankles so swollen her legs go straight down from her calves. She's back a minute later with a plate and chips for us.

"You didn't have to do that," I say while filling the last pepper shaker.

"I know, but it sounded good to me, too."

I dig in, not realizing how starved I am. Desiree takes a few tastes but mostly sits with a peaceful Madonna expression on her face. I'm thankful she didn't ask a bunch of questions.

About eight, the restaurant fills up. John throws together sandwiches in the back while Desiree shuttles orders between tables and the kitchen, even though moving around is difficult for her. Finally, I can't stand watching her from my spot in the back. When one table of four leaves, I hop up and hurry over to bus the table.

Desiree breezes by me with three wicker baskets of food. "You don't have to do that."

"I know." But I seat the next group that walks in and hand out menus, anyway. How could I sit on my butt while she's running around? That'd be so, so wrong. By the end of the night, I figure out Desiree's number system for coding tables and I deliver orders, refill drinks and bus tables for her. When the rush is over, she sits at the back table and rests her feet on the milk crate while I keep the few remaining tables serviced, deliver their checks and spiff up the dining room.

John finishes cleaning the kitchen while I lock the door behind the last party. It's 11:30 when I climb into the backseat of the Toyota.

Desiree twists halfway in the seat, resting her arm on the headrest. She holds a wad of cash in her hand. "It's some of the tips. For you." I shake my head but she says, "Take it. You earned it. You were a huge help."

I'll need this for living expenses. Tentatively, I take the cash, mostly ones, and whisper an embarrassed thanks.

~~~

Bob Dylan greets us the minute we walk into their apartment. John grabs the leash to walk him.

Desiree says, "You can have the guest room."

The room she mentioned is really a junk room—stacked with the baby stuff Mom and I bought, books piled on the desk and open boxes filled with odds and ends. I toss my duffle bag amongst the other stuff.

"This is going to be the nursery." Desiree moves some ratty bath towels and a few of John's old trophies off the couch and then opens it. Then she waddles to the closet and grabs linens.

If this were my house, the room would already be painted, decorated and off-limits.

"I can make it." Because I want her to get off her feet.

Desiree watches as I flip sheets this way and that, making up the sofa bed in a style that would pass military muster—the old, *will a coin bounce?* trick.

"The bath is down the hall." She hands me one of the old towels. "Do you need something to sleep in?"

When I nod, she waves a c'mon motion. As we pass through the apartment, Dylan follows us, tail wagging. John's back from walking him and playing phone messages.

*Beep.* "Hi, John. It's Mom. Give me a call."

*Beep.* "Hi, John. It's me again. I'm wondering if you've heard anything from Jane."

*Beep.* "John? Mom. It's ten p.m., and Jane's not home yet. I'm hoping she's with you."

*Beep.* "John or Desiree—whoever gets this—please call me.

It doesn't matter what time."

I feel a little guilty about not answering any of her calls to my cell, but not so guilty that I want to call her back.

John ruffles my hair. It's a gesture from when I was a lot shorter than him. "I'll call her. You need to get some sleep. School tomorrow."

I'd packed everything but my nightshirt, so Desiree gives me an old team jersey of John's. I'll be sleeping like I belong with the Trophy-Casers.

In my room—or rather, Lily's room—I slip into the shirt and start crying. It's not a big, wailing cry, but the kind where slow, quiet tears leak from your eyes. Crawling into bed, I tuck myself in and pull the covers tight to my chin.

Plop, plop.

Suddenly I remember something I forgot—Flipper. This brings a huge lump to my throat. Could I feel any worse?

Bob Dylan nudges the partially open door, pads into the room and rests his chin on the mattress. He snuffles my face, licks my cheek. And after consoling me, he curls up next to the sofa bed and lets loose a huge sigh that sounds like, *It will get better, Jane. Eventually.*

# CHAPTER TWENTY-ONE

The best thing about hanging by the water fountain is everyone gets thirsty at some point. This morning it's Travis.

He stands outside my pod looking for a way through. Ordinarily, we'd part like the Red Sea, but today Lexie and Lucas are talking loudly, ignoring him. Travis better return with Moses if he wants a drink.

Finally, he clears his throat several times and taps Lexie on the shoulder. She turns and the way she stares at him you'd think he's some kind of insect. "Oh, hi Travis. I didn't see you. What do you want?"

"Some water?" Travis shifts from foot to foot.

Lexie moves out of his way and grabs me. She pushes me directly behind him as he bends over the fountain. My heart and head pound. I don't want anything to do with this liar. When I try to back away, Lexie won't let me budge.

Okay. Fine. It might be good to get this over with.

Travis finishes, spins around and runs smack into me.

"Do do…do do." I sing the *Jaws* music and make the shark fin on my head.

Travis laughs nervously.

"You lied." I'm so proud for not being wimpy.

Travis sways, clears his throat, rubs his nose. "Oh yeah. Well, sorry. But I'm a chick magnet, y'know. Had to maintain my rep."

I think Travis has forgotten ninth grade science. "Magnets can repel, too," I remind him.

His mouth drops open. "I wanted to make Alana jealous."

"How's *that* workin' out for you?" The thumping in my chest is still beating machine gun fast.

Travis squirms and it makes me feel better. "Not the way I thought." He looks at the ground.

A surge of anger. It's not about the lie; it's about the result. "Do you even realize you pushed them together? Do you?"

Travis looks up from the ground and his mouth flops open like a fish. A completely dumbfounded fish. "I didn't mean to."

Yeah. I bet. This is a half-assed apology by a jumbo-sized asshole, but it's the best I'm going to get. I let him pass.

~~~

Two days later, I'm shocked to see Irwin with Lexie.

"Lucas will be here in a minute," she says to him. Willow cruises up and Lexie says, "Hey, girl. Do you know Tad?"

"Hi, Tad." Willow leans against the wall in her usual location.

Lexie faces me. "I had to do something to counteract all your moping."

Typical. She's about five steps ahead of me. I have no idea what she's talking about.

"My moping?"

"Yeah. It's time for you to raise yourself out of that funk and I know what will do it." She pauses. "A hunt."

*Oh, that would be fun!*

Finally, Irwin looks in my direction and smiles. "I'm waiting for Lucas. I understand until now he's always been the Master of the Scavenger Hunts."

Lucas was the original brain behind the hunts. His sense of humor always gave them their *special* quality.

"Why? Is he not in charge this time?"

"Because Irwin—I mean, Tad—is going to do it," Lexie explains.

I scowl at her in the way you can only do with your best friend and she reads my confusion. Perfectly. "We're taking it school-wide this time."

"Oh no." I laugh.

"Oh yes. And this is your chance to settle everything with Alana. Sam will be the trophy."

When I glance over my shoulder, Alana watches us from her spot by the glass case.

"Once everyone knows about the hunt, I hope this doesn't look as if we're cheating," Willow says.

"If Irwin does a good job on the list, everyone will know there's no way to cheat," Lexie says.

Irwin will probably make an awesome judge. "I'm glad you're here," I tell him.

"It's only because of the scavenger hunt. I still prefer the darkroom."

For some reason this makes me laugh. "That's cool."

Lucas strolls up and hands Irwin a sheaf of papers. "All the past hunts. This should give you a pretty good feel for the rules and the kinds of tasks."

Irwin flips through the sheets and snickers. "You can't even do all these. What does this mean—*Pass the point of no return – 15 pts.*?"

"We never made a list that could be completed. You'll be surprised. Some of those get funky, creative interpretations, but we always include a few *impossible* items. Just have fun with it. Go wild."

Irwin pushes his glasses up the bridge of his nose. "Wild?"

"Yeah," Lexie agrees. "The weirder, the better."

"You just gotta make sure there is something that's good for everyone," Lucas says.

Irwin's brows knit in confusion.

"What he means is have an item for every pod," I explain. Irwin definitely gets the pod thing. We've discussed it at length in the darkroom. "Something intellectual for the science lab pod. Something athletic for the trophy case."

Irwin nods and continues to flip through the papers, laughing out loud, despite himself.

~~~

By Friday, we've talked to Nigel, Karen Perry and Brendan/Brandon. They're all in. Only the trophy case is not involved. Lexie wants them included so we can *kick some Alana Atwood booty* is the way she put it. I'm kinda hoping to avoid that confrontation altogether.

So, naturally, before the first bell, Sam gets thirsty while I'm standing next to the fountain. He presses cool fingertips to the back of my neck, before he stoops low to get a drink. His touch makes my knees wobble.

He takes a step closer and says in a low voice, "I wanted to let you know—Travis and I talked last night."

This comment could mean any one of a thousand things. That they spoke about school or sports, their favorite band, but the way Sam's dark brown eyes don't leave mine—I'm pretty sure he means they discussed me.

"And?" I ask.

"He told me the truth. And I still don't get it, but I know that you didn't—I mean Travis made us all think that a lot more happened."

This is an impossible conversation. I mean, we're in the main hall before school starts for cryin' out loud. I wish we still had lunches together, because there's a lot I'd like to talk to him about.

Shifting my backpack from one shoulder to the other, I say, "I'm not proud of the fact that I kissed Travis." My eyes are telegraphing *I'm sorry, so sorry.* Sam blushes and bends to take another swig from the fountain. In my head I lean over him and tell him, *The whole time I thought of you.*

He stands and wipes a little water from his mouth with the back of his hand. "How much have you read for Breckenridge's class?"

I'd finished the whole play before we'd been assigned this scene. "All of it."

"Maybe we should rehearse. You could come to my house, or I could go to yours?"

*Alana would not like that one little bit.*

Maybe he read my mind because Sam looks over his shoulder at her and back at me, waiting for an answer.

"I don't drive yet and probably can't get a ride to your house. I'm staying with my brother and his wife right now. They live over by the mall."

If we still ate lunches together, Sam would have known this whole deal. But this is news to him. Once again, we're into a subject that isn't great for the main hall.

There's so much to tell. Like how John convinced Mom to let things sort themselves out, or how I don't have someone on my back all the time, or how their apartment is more cluttered than my bedroom has ever been. Life with them is easygoing and a little messy, but the world hasn't stopped turning on its axis. Yet.

Sam gives me a look—quizzical and concerned. "I can drive there, but why aren't you at your house?"

I lean my backpack against the wall, hoping to be swallowed whole.

*Can I change the subject?*

That's when help arrives from an unexpected source. Alana strolls up and says, "How are you, Jane?" which is a normal, everyday greeting. Except the pitch of her voice makes it sound more like, *Hey bitch! Quit talking to my boyfriend.*

"Good," I reply. "We were just talking about getting together to rehearse for our scene from *Romeo and Juliet*."

Sam takes a quick breath. Alana narrows her eyes at me, then wraps both arms around his waist. "I hear you guys are having a hunt for the whole school."

I shrug.

"Yeah, well I'll just get the scoop from Irwin in Yearbook."

She just assumes they're included. Of course they are. They're the Trophy-Casers. The bell rings and Alana practically pulls Sam from his spot, which takes quite a lot of strength because he's a big guy. As they walk away, Alana grabs his hand and I can overhear her. "You don't need to rehearse with *her*. Breckenridge will let you read from the book."

Oh, Lexie is so right. They have to be in it.

Sam drops her hand and yells back to me over the tops of all the heads between us. "How's next Tuesday? I'll come to your brother's."

*Wow. If this was the Scavenger Hunt, I'd probably get points for that.*

# CHAPTER TWENTY–TWO

Desiree inhales deeply, straightens her spine and slowly lifts her arms over her head. Her enormous belly hangs over her skinny outstretched legs that end with puffy ankles. She hasn't tied her hair back, and it fluffs around her tranquil Renaissance Madonna face as she does her evening pre-natal yoga. For a minute her hair and legs make me think of Bob Dylan, who's curled in the corner.

She holds the pose while John rummages around for books, folders and pens he needs for his night course at FAU. He's running late.

I sprawl on the couch, depressed, and tap his leg as he passes me. "I don't get it." I'm talking about the quadratic formula.

"I never got it either," Desiree pulls her hands down into a prayer position in the middle of her chest.

"It's like any other equation," John says.

This is no help. It's exactly what Mrs. Fonseca says to the class. If it's just like every other equation, why do so many kids struggle? Why do people have to keep saying that copout answer? If it were, they wouldn't say that.

"It's not," I tell John. "I've solved algebra equations since the eighth grade."

"I can't help you tonight. Sorry. I've got class, but tomorrow I'll sit with you. Okay?"

Desiree crisscrosses her legs. "Don't stress. The quadratic formula will have absolutely no bearing on your life. I haven't used it since I left high school."

I'm glad I won't have to keep using it, but still, I want to pass Algebra.

"Let it go," she says.

"Where's my text?" John spins around and almost runs over Desiree as she sits up and lifts her arms high over her head.

She moves in slow motion. "Take a deep breath, hon. It'll appear."

Their apartment is totally chaotic compared to the way Mom keeps the house. There are times, for instance when I'm getting ready for school in the morning, that I miss the organization.

John sighs, and then finds his book under a pile of maternity bras on a chair with clean laundry. He frowns at

Desiree in a way that reminds me of Mom. It's so hard to break from nineteen years of indoctrination.

"I told you it works." Desiree folds her body as flat as she can with her little belly.

This makes John laugh and shake his head. "Tomorrow. I promise." He leans over and kisses my forehead, then stoops over and kisses Desiree on the lips.

She keeps her eyes closed and says, "Mmmmm…hurry back."

After John leaves, she uses the edge of the chair to hoist herself off the floor. "Let me show you something." She reaches for a magazine from a basket by the chair and opens it to a dog-eared page of a floral garden that is overgrown and wild. It reminds me of a Crayola 64 version of the preserve. "Could you paint this in the nursery?"

The reminder that we're less than three weeks from the baby's arrival twists in my stomach. What will I do after she arrives?

I study the picture. It would be challenging to paint all those little flowers in a semi-Impressionistic style. "I think so," I say.

"Good. Then that will be your rent."

I burst into tears. Partly because I don't have enough money to really pay my own way and also because I don't know what's in store for me—with anything.

"You can stay as long as you need," Desiree says.

"It's not just that. It's everything. School, friends—" I break off with a sniffle.

"Your Mom?"

"Yeah."

"A guy?"

I can't believe she figured it out. "How did you know?"

"I was sixteen once. Let's talk Mom first."

I want Desiree—no, change that—I *need* Desiree to understand how bound Mom makes me feel. "She disapproves of so much. Like your job. She said once she doesn't want me to end up a waitress the way you did."

Desiree laughs. "That won't happen."

How can she laugh? "How do you know?"

"Because I'm not a waitress. I own the Organic Cornucopia."

Wow! Shut my mouth. Shut Mom's too.

"Sorry," I manage. "I didn't know."

"No biggie." She sighs. "Let's talk about the guy. That might be an easier fix." Desiree says this like she expects me to spill and despite myself, I do.

I tell her everything about Sam. From meeting him to the day in the parking lot when Alana ambushed us. I tell her about Rodeo Bob's, dancing with Sam and Irwin getting sick. I almost skip the part about the beach, but she gets that out of me too.

Through it all, she keeps saying, "I see. Then what?"

And I keep talking, pouring it out. I tell her about returning to school and how Sam thought I'd screwed around with Travis and how he ended up with Alana. And now, the Scavenger Hunt.

"That's an interesting way to settle things." She laughs.

"I know." And that's when I tell her Sam might come by tomorrow night.

Finally, I take a deep breath and stop. It's like I've been talking for days and I'm ready for a rest. Lexie knows all this, but she's been living it with me. Somehow, telling the whole story at one time is therapy.

"Do you want to hear what I think?" She pats my leg.

I'm not sure I do. I ran away from my Mom and don't need or want Mom-sounding advice.

She waits for my answer.

"I guess so."

She takes a deep breath. "I think this guy, Sam, cares about you. And I think you need to apologize to him. I understand why you kissed that other guy—what's his name?"

"Travis?"

"Yeah, Travis. I understand why you kissed him. You know you shouldn't have, but I get it."

I'm nodding.

"But I think you hurt Sam's feelings. So when he comes here tomorrow—and I'm glad it's tomorrow because John and I have the day off again—you need to come clean."

I nod, swiping at a tear.

"Listen." She rubs my shoulder. "You're not the first person who's made a mistake, and you won't be the last." She shifts her hand to her belly and palms it like a crystal ball. "And I think if he comes over, everything's going to be all right."

I wish I could rub her belly too, so I could see what Sam will do when I try my best to apologize.

~~~

"Janey, there's someone at the front door for you," John yells through my door.

Sam? Sam! "Who?" I yell back, like I'm so popular and a ton of people besides Lexie pop in to see me.

"Someone named Sam."

My heart leaps to my throat. I wasn't sure he'd come. Wasn't sure Alana would let him. Still, I tried on four outfits earlier for Desiree, just in case. After all that drama I ended up in my favorite jean shorts and a tee.

I step from my room. Sam stands in the foyer. John and Desiree are on the couch. This apartment is so small it redefines cozy.

The doorbell must have woken Bob Dylan, because all of a sudden he rounds the corner at top speed. He gives Sam the sniff-and-greet treatment. Sam steps back, astonished.

"He likes you," Desiree says.

Yeah, so do I, but that's not how I say "hi" to Sam. "Dylan! Stop!" I say, and he does. He's amazingly well-behaved once he gets past the greeting.

Sam pats Dylan on his head, racking up more brownie points with me. He must be at a gazillion by now.

While I break up the Sam-Dylan tryst, Desiree and John snuggle on the sofa. Desiree rests her head on John's chest, her legs tucked under, belly pooched out.

"Hey," I say to Sam. "This is my brother John and his wife Desiree. They're having a baby." This is probably obvious. I mean, Desiree's stomach is enormous. "And this is Sam." I resemble a game show hostess with the way I wave my hands around.

Desiree gives me a quick, almost imperceptible wink.

Some people would act surprised about the baby or their age difference. To Sam's credit, he doesn't even flinch. "Nice to meet you," he says in his friendly, open way and shakes John's hand and then Desiree's.

"Do I know you?" John asks, shifting on the couch.

"I don't think so."

"Right. I don't think I've ever met you, but you look really familiar. Weird." John shrugs his shoulders.

"When's the baby due?" Sam asks Desiree.

"March fourteenth."

Sam sits on a chair, folds his hands and leans in. "Oh! That's soon. Did you take Lamaze?"

"You know about Lamaze?" Desiree asks.

I'm surprised too. Will I ever know everything about Sam?

"My cousin had a baby about a year ago, and sometimes I'd practice with her."

"Really?" Desiree raises her eyebrows and smiles, challenging him.

"I did," Sam insists. "I know how to breathe. Watch. Hee, hee, whoooooo."

Desiree laughs. "You do know how to breathe." She breathes with him. "Hee, hee, whoooooo." They're panting in unison, and it cracks John and me up. Suddenly she stops and asks Sam, "Did your cousin use it? Lamaze, I mean?"

"She tried, but decided to use drugs."

"I know. That worries me. It's like you want to do the right thing, and then you're overwhelmed by the situation and emotions." Desiree rests her hands on her tummy. "People. Sometimes we're not strong enough."

I know Desiree is talking about labor, but it feels like she's talking about what I did at the beach or how I need to come clean.

During the exchange, Sam's eyebrows arch, and he rests his tongue on his chipped tooth. I want to say, *That's what happened to me.*

Desiree lounges on the couch. It's so strange she's a dog person because she moves feline, slow and fluid. She smiles like she just had several helpings of canary at the all-you-can-eat bird buffet.

She pats her belly as if to say, *Well, my job's done*, and grabs John by the hand. "We should move to the other room. These guys gotta study." She smiles at me as she leads John out.

Sam scoots off the chair and sits beside me on the floor, our backs pressed against the sofa. He rubs his cheek. "She's really nice."

"Yeah. She is. We talked about you."

"Me?"

"Yeah. I told her all about the Snow Ball and stuff. Y'know, I should never have kissed Travis at the beach. It's what Desiree was saying—the emotions messed with my head." Sam starts to interrupt but I put my hand up near his mouth to silence him. "Let me finish, okay? You don't know this about me, but until that night I'd never kissed anyone."

Sam looks surprised.

"I know." I snicker. "It's pathetic. Have you kissed someone?" Of course he has. What kind of question is that? I laugh at myself. "Don't answer. That was a dumb question. But if you hadn't kissed someone, wouldn't you be desperate to try it? You might even kiss—" I try hard to come up with a bizarre name. "Becca Chartrand." She's an odd girl, stranger than me, actually, who mutters to herself as she walks through the halls and every so often has angry conversations with people who aren't there.

Sam snorts. "Probably not Becca. But I get what you mean."

"And then you weren't at the beach. Or at least I thought you weren't. I thought you were with Alana somewhere. I mean, you were with Alana, but I mean *with*-with."

"I see." Sam nods, then adds, "You worry too much about Alana."

What he's saying hits the bull's-eye and I know it's true. She bothers me. It's the fact that we used to be friends, but I'm not good enough for her. And she doesn't think I'm good enough for Sam. And in a really screwed-up way, I sort of believe she's right. It's like we're competing for Sam and maybe the Hunt is our way of settling it.

I've been totally honest up to this point, but then I say, "It's okay if you like her. I just want us to be friends again." My big, fat lie—I still want Sam as a boyfriend.

"We are friends. In fact, we're Romeo and Juliet." He holds up his copy of the play with one hand and rests the other on the floor by my hip. "We should rehearse, huh?"

It's the closest we've been since our dance and I don't know how I'll be able to think.

With my book open to Act Three, Scene Five, I watch every

move Sam makes. I don't actually need the book, because after Breckenridge assigned the scene, I read it twenty or thirty times. It's the last time they speak and about halfway through, they kiss.

Fortunately, or maybe unfortunately, Breckenridge already solved this issue for me. During the party scene near the end of Act I, Romeo kisses Juliet twice. When Connor and Emily performed for the class last week, they were going to really kiss and Breckenridge said, "Kissing her hand will do, thank you."

So I'd decided when we get to the kiss, I'll hold out my hand for Sam.

His leg bounces in time to the music playing in the other room. As we read, his leg grazes mine every couple of beats. It's way more distracting than his chipped tooth. We're coming to the kiss and I read, "Then, window, let day in and let life out."

"Farewell, farewell. One kiss and I'll descend."

As Sam leans in, Desiree walks into the room. He jerks away like we got caught kissing.

"Oops. Sorry. Just getting some ice cream. Do you guys want anything?"

Sam says *no* while my mouth runs away. "I want a lot of things. But no thanks to the ice cream."

Desiree giggles, gets bowls for her and John and returns to their room.

Sam's face is inches from mine, hovering. "What do you want?" he asks softly.

A million thoughts run through my head, but I can't find the right words so it's quiet for a long, long time.

"What?" Sam whispers.

I ignore him and read my next lines.

"Wait!" Sam says, and bends over to kiss my temple.

There is absolutely no debate, no question, no doubt about what I want. I want more.

~~~

Later on, after Sam's gone home, there's a light tap on my bedroom door. John opens it and peeks inside. "I figured out who he was. I knew I'd seen him before."

"How do you know Sam?"

"I don't know him." John points to the sketch of Sam that I brought from home. I'd hung it on the wall here. "God, Jane. That's really good. I saw you draw that—when was it?"

"The day you told Mom and Dad about Desiree."

"That's right. I forgot." John leans forward to eye the sketch closely. "You've liked him for a long time, huh?"

I shrug. "When did you figure it out?"

"All of a sudden it hit me where I'd seen him, so I grilled Desiree to see if she knew anything. That guy, he likes you."

"You're just saying that."

"No. No, I'm not. I'm a guy, and I know how guys act. I

know how I acted."

I avoid John's eyes and flip the pages of *Romeo and Juliet*. "He's in the trophy case pod."

"So was I," John says. "Sometimes that doesn't matter."

He's out the door and it's practically shut when John says through the crack, "Tomorrow night. Algebra tutoring. I didn't forget."

I had. And it's good he postponed. I glance from the book to the drawing and smile at Sam's sketched face, replaying his lips against my temple over and over and over again.

# CHAPTER TWENTY-THREE

Last night the frame in the sofa bed poked me in the back again and I didn't get enough sleep. I'm living some weird variation of the Princess and the Pea. Except I'm not a princess, and the pea is an old sofa bed that needs a thicker mattress.

So, I'm cranky.

But not only from lack of sleep. Because after Sam studied with me earlier this week and we talked about the Snow Ball and Travis and everything, I thought things would be different at school. They're not. He and Alana are as cozy as ever.

To top it off, Lexie's deserted me today at lunch. She has a dentist appointment, so I can't even really be mad at her.

Slouching through the line, I sling a sandwich onto my tray.

"Hey, if Dakota Fanning married Oliver North," a voice from behind me says.

My heart skips three beats. "Dakota North! That doesn't

make sense."

"Yeah, but it's funny when you fill out forms." He smiles, and I make a weak attempt at one. We always had funny, smart conversations without some big point.

Sam grabs a slice of pizza. Then another. And another.

"Shoot! Just take the whole pizza, would ya?"

He laughs and slides his tray along the silver rails toward the register. "Where's Lexie?"

"Dentist. It's worse than cafeteria food."

Sam laughs again. "We should eat together."

"Where's Alana?" My voice is frosty.

"She called in sick today. Trying to get some extra sleep before The Hunt, y'know? "

This fuels my already crappy mood. I'm pissed Alana's mom is lax about stuff like that. Would my mom ever let me take a day off? No way. But the worse thing is the way Sam's using me as a lunch buddy substitute.

"Yeah, whatever." I sniff. I don't know what's gotten into me. I'd swear it's PMS, but it's the wrong time of the month. More likely it's BMS—Bad Mattress Syndrome.

I follow Sam to our old table and sit across from him. Two tables over I see Willow give me a curious look, then a grin, while everyone at Sam's table stares openly. He squeezes the wedge on his milk carton, smiling, like he's happy to be here. When he rests his tongue against his chipped tooth, my hostility fades. A bit.

As we sit together, I have a déjà vu vibe. It's like all our lunches earlier this year, but not exactly because so much has happened since then. The Snow Ball. Travis' lie. Our conversation the other night. A small kiss from Sam. Why did he ask me what I wanted? Was he just teasing me? It didn't feel that way.

"So Lexie's at the dentist."

I'm startled and say *yeah*, with finality, killing the conversation before it starts.

"How's John?"

"Good."

"How's Desiree? She's close, huh?"

"March fourteenth."

Honestly, I don't know why I'm doing this. You'd think I'd be happy to have lunch with him.

"So, are you excited about The Hunt tomorrow?"

When he asks this, I get annoyed. Not a little irate like I'd been until now, but major domo pissed. Doesn't he know Alana and I are competing. Over him. There's a lot more at stake than some stupid Hunt. Him. My home. My life. Doesn't he get that?

I answer his question with a question. "Are you my friend?"

"What? Janey! You know we're friends."

"Then how can you be so clueless about this? I'm living at my brother's with a baby on the way. I don't even know where

I'll be sleeping next month. Do you think I care about the Hunt?"

That sounds a little overly dramatic, even to me. But, too bad—it's how I feel.

Sam looks at his tray and says, "I know. But I thought you were into it. I thought you and your friends came up with the idea."

I glare at him. "Well, we did. Come up with it. But that was before. I might not even do it."

Lexie and company would kill me if I backed out now. My pod might not care about winning this thing, but they don't want to lose to the Trophy-Casers.

"Sorry. I didn't know."

I smoosh my tuna sandwich into my plate. "Well now you do."

"Listen, I'm just trying to make conversation with you," Sam says, palms up. "You're not making it easy."

I raise an eyebrow.

"I mean, you haven't asked me one question," Sam says.

He's wrong. I asked him if he was my friend, but I know what he means. It's just I'm sick of his flirting not being any more than that. And I'm sick of Alana getting in the way. But what really gets me is the whole cross-clique taboo that keeps everyone from dating anyone outside the socially acceptable circle. The whole trophy case, water fountain, science lab, courtyard pod thing.

"Here's a question for you. Do you go out with Alana because she's in your pod or because you're too spineless to end it?"

Sam's mouth drops open.

"She's not a nice person, in case you hadn't noticed," I continue, "And, and...she's got a lousy of sense of humor. I bet she wouldn't even get your Oliver North/Dakota Fanning joke and I know she'd never come up with one. I don't get it. She's not even good-looking."

So the last insult I hurled is a humongous lie, because she's gorgeous and everyone knows it.

Sam laughs at my tirade, which infuriates me. My anger and jealousy are like a dolphin that's been trapped in a fishing net and finally surfaces. I can't push it under until it gets what it needs—breathing room.

"Because I don't know which is worse, that you're too worried about what other people think, or that you let this carry you along, not taking any action when you want to. Because if you told the truth, Sam—if you told the truth to yourself and the world—you like me. You like me a lot more than Alana, but I'm not 'cool.' I know I'm a little out there, but you must be a little out there too because you like me more." My voice drops to a whisper because all the anger inside collapsed. "And I don't know which hurts worse. That you're with Alana or that I care you're with her."

Sam stares at his plate and pushes crumbs around with his pizza crust, while I wish I could take back every word.

His mouth flattens into a thin angry line, but that emotion doesn't make it to his eyes. The brown eyes are sad. And am I imagining it, or do I see guilt?

I sigh massively. "Sorry," I croak. I mean the word in so many ways. Sorry I'd gotten angry. Sorry I'd been mean. Sorry I'd said these words at all.

Sam grabs me by the wrist and looks at me intently. "I never meant to hurt anyone, and I still don't want to." He drops my wrist. "Especially you." Then he picks up his tray and walks away.

I watch him leave. And do nothing.

I meant the words I said to Sam. Everything about the way he acts says he prefers me—the Snow Ball set up, the sweet kiss when we rehearsed. I've never even seen him kiss Alana. And they're supposed to be a couple.

So, if I'm right that means Sam is too afraid of hurting Alana and maybe too afraid of what his trophy case friends would think if he actually dated me. It's weak and I deserve to be treated better. I do. The problem with that? I like him anyway. The way I feel—in fact, this entire situation—is out of my control. It's like this fast current is carrying me in a direction I don't want to go.

And tomorrow's Hunt will be out of control, too. The only thing left to do is to go with the flow.

*Dolphins have no physical home. To a dolphin, "home" is wherever pod-mates are.*

*(Excerpt:* The Magic and Mystery of Dolphins*)*

# CHAPTER TWENTY-FOUR

I'm wearing Dolphin Girl.

At the Macy's entrance to the mall, I look through the costume's mouth. All I see is The Gap and Hallmark cards on the left, The Loft and Musicland on the right. Straight ahead is a crowd of people milling around.

Less than two minutes ago, we completed our first check-in with Irwin.

Earlier, Lexie said, "Let's start with easy stuff. Look at number twelve. You could wear your dolphin costume. We'll do it right after check-in."

*Easy? Yeah. Sure. Easy for you.*

But it's worth thirty points, so there's no sense standing around. I take off running, my dorsal fin flopping around as I try to avoid a lady pushing a stroller.

Lucas keeps pace with me to film this task. To be honest, he looks as ridiculous as I do. He's wearing transvestite-quality make-up, and Lexie's spiked his hair three inches off his head. Items #21 and #22.

Weaving through shoppers, I take tiny, quick steps because the bottom of the costume is incredibly narrow. It would have been impossible to dance in. Lexie, Willow and Tara follow, laughing hysterically, which gets Lucas and me started. I'm more than halfway there, running past Pac Sun.

*Don't get distracted. Keep going.*

As I pass Godiva, turning right into the food court, I nearly run over Ashley and Alana and have to skirt around them. They're holding their phones open toward the main entrance. And who steps through the door? Sam in his Speedo and goggles.

Nice. He looks waaay better than me.

~~~

We end up at Willow's house after completing item # 7— something wild and out of control. We doubled the speed limit near a deserted playground. Lucas took phone footage of the sign—10 mph—and then trained his phone on the odometer until it read "20 mph" while Lexie shrieked, "We're wild. We're out of control!"

They head to the garage, arguing Barney vs. The Wiggles, to perform item # 31. I know they won't need me on this task, so I wander into the house's den. This is the kind of room I could settle into immediately, every wall lined with books and overstuffed, comfy couches.

Standing in front of the shelves, I survey all the titles and then spot a row of *Chicken Soup* books. "Hey Willow! You guys have *Chicken Soup*," I holler toward the garage where they're setting up.

"Oh, I know," she says wistfully, "But my mom loves those books and she'd kill me if we shredded the pages."

Lexie marches over and grabs the book from my hands. "We have to make soup with this, Willow."

"She'll kill me."

"We'll buy her a new book."

"Why can't we just buy one now?"

"Because," Lexie says like she's explaining to a child, "Amazon does not teleport paper books. Doesn't your mom have a Kindle?" Willow shrugs while Lexie juggles the book back and forth. "Sorry. This one is being sacrificed for the greater good."

Willow covers her eyes as Lexie rips three or four pages

from the book and starts tearing them into strips. "Look! Noodles." Lexie finds a pot under the counter and adds the book noodles. They flutter into the pot. Then she raids the pantry for a can of chicken soup, grabbing the opener. "Film this, Lucas."

She stirs the mixture as Lucas films, takes the spoon and sips it. "Mmmm. I feel better already."

It's because we just earned fifty points.

"On to the next." Lexie rinses the soup and some of the book down the disposal as Willow finally uncovers her eyes. "Jane, we need your vote to break the tie. 'You Are Special' by Barney, or 'Fruit Salad' by The Wiggles?"

No contest. I love the purple dinosaur.

~~~

While I pick pieces of peanut from Tara's hair, a side effect of her Herbal Essences experience before we left Willow's house, the team debates our next task. Poor Tara. All Willow had in her pantry was chunky. I wipe the peanut butter residue on my shorts and say, "Let me see the list."

There are a couple things that would be easy that we haven't done yet: #14 and #51. Then I get a great idea. "Let's do number twenty-three—pet a cow. It's worth fifty points."

"Okay," Tara says. "But how far way are those farms?"

Lucas pipes up. "Twenty minutes. Sorry, Jane, I think it'll

take too long to get there."

"But we're only five minutes from The Shoppes. There's that big ceramic statue outside The Sacred Cow." It's this funky consignment shop everyone loves. I hand the list to Lucas.

"You're a genius," he says, and Lexie makes a U-turn at the next light.

When we pull into the center and cruise past Burger King, Willow says, "Look. The Dudes."

Nigel Chang and his friends sit in the kiddie area, tossing colored balls from the play pit at each other and laughing.

"Let's stop for a minute," I suggest. We park and walk to a fence that separates the parking lot from the restaurant. Hanging over the fence, I say, "Hey Nige! How's the hunt goin'?"

"*Bien*, Jane. Doin' *bien*." He flips his long, black bangs away from his face. "We just got three-hundred points." Justin tosses a yellow ball and it hits the back of Nigel's head. He laughs.

"Wow," I say. "For what?"

Nigel puts his elbows on the picnic table in front of him. "We got the munchies and Andre's good at math, so we consumed ten-thousand calories...times three."

Andre gives his stomach a pat.

I look at Nigel. "You ate thirty-thousand calories?"

"Almost. I'm still working on this." Nigel holds up jumbo-sized shake.

I chuckle. Lexie laughs outright and pretty soon we're all

hysterical—even Nigel.

He sort of hiccups. "What's so funny?"

Lexie shakes her head. "You were supposed to eat at McDonald's, not BK."

"Aw, man." Nigel calmly takes a sip of his shake. "I told you guys Mickey D's."

The rest of the courtyard pod thinks this is as funny as my friends do. They double over, laughing. Nigel picks up a blue ball and tosses it at Andre. "Look at us. Now we have to go bribe the judge."

This cracks me up. "Good luck bribing Irwin," I tell him. I figure these guys need all the help they can get at this point. "Did you know you can pet a cow over there?" I point at the entrance to The Sacred Cow. "Plus, you get extra points for my assistance."

"Cool. Thanks. See ya." Nigel mentions this to Andre, slurps the last of the shake and gives his stomach a rub-a-dub.

~~~

At the second check-in, I hand Irwin a cup of Coldstone and tease, "Hope you enjoy it, *Tad*."

Irwin smiles and digs in.

"Did we make you happy?" I ask. Because that's item #33 and worth fifty points.

Irwin smirks as he pulls the clean spoon from his mouth. "Not yet."

"Well, are we at least winning?" Lexie asks.

"Nope. The Dudes are in first with six-hundred twenty points. The Champs are second with five-hundred eighty-five. You're in third with five-hundred fifty." Irwin shovels in more ice cream, and we cruise off.

Nigel didn't need help as much as I thought.

"I don't care if we lose," Lexie says as we head to the Jeep. "I just don't want Alana to beat us."

Even Willow agrees. At the other end of the center from the checkpoint is a Wendy's. Lucas has volunteered to drink Wendy's chicken nugget sauce—if we tackle the first part and secure them.

"We're going to need to buy nuggets," Willow says.

"Not necessarily." Lexie parks the Jeep.

Inside she heads straight to the counter, while Lucas finds us a table. Right before I sit across from Lucas, I notice Sam at a small table against the window with a pile of sauce packets in front of him, most of them empty. A small drawstring bag hangs on the back of his seat.

I slide into the seat across from him. "You looked good at the mall."

He grins and snorts. "Yeah. Not as good as you."

I guess he did see me.

Lucas moves our table closer to Sam's. Lexie joins him with a tray piled with packets. She gets a bit sniffy. I guess she's still upset with him.

Sam hunches over his packets, drawing close to me. "Hey, I want to talk to you about our lunch last week," he says in a low voice.

"Me too," I say. "I'm so sorry I yelled at you. If you want to be with Alana, it's okay." I don't know why I'm saying this, but I am telling the truth this time. "Look, I got jealous, but you're a person, not some trophy. I do like you—a lot—but it's more important to have you as a friend."

Sam grabs my hand. "Here's the thing—"

"What's goin' on?" Lexie interrupts as she opens packets for Lucas.

What was he going to say?

Sam rests his tongue on the chipped tooth, then waves his hand over the pile in front of him. "I'm consuming a lot of nugget sauce," he says, which makes us laugh.

"Where's the rest of your team?" Lexie asks.

"I think I lost them."

"What?" I say.

"Yeah. Alana didn't want me to eat the sauce in her car, so they left me here to go pet the statue at The Sacred Cow."

Crap! They thought of the cow, too? Who came up with it? Probably Alana, because we used to go there in middle school.

What a kick in the ass.

"How long have they been gone?"

Sam looks at his waterproof watch. "More than thirty minutes."

Lexie and I give each other a *that's-strange* look because they should have come back for him by now. Maybe they decided to do something else near that center.

"Well, come sit with us while you wait," I say.

Sam brings the unopened packets to our table and says to Lucas, "Want these? I can't do anymore."

Lucas tears back the cover from another packet of honey mustard. "Maybe."

Sam saunters back to his table and Lexie raises her eyebrows at me. He stuffs the empty, sticky packets into his front pocket then shrugs. "It's proof," he mumbles.

"Yeah, good thinking," Lucas says.

I grin at Sam. "You just helped us, y'know. We get points for that." I fold my arms on the table and face my pod. "If they don't come for him, we should take him," I say. "We can't leave him sitting here."

"I don't know," Lexie bites her cuticle. "Do you think it's a trick or something? If we take him, they get forty points."

"If it's not a trick, wouldn't you feel bad leaving him?"

Lexie doesn't answer and only chews on her finger some more until Lucas wipes his lips with the back of his hand and says, "He should come with us."

Ten minutes later, Lucas has consumed fifteen of the twenty packets and the rest of Sam's pod hasn't shown up.

"One more gives us the max points," I say.

"You're so good at math," Willow says.

"Yeah, just don't ask me to do the quadratic formula."

Lucas finishes the sixteenth packet and sips on a Sprite Lexie bought for him. "Do you want to come with us or keep waiting for them?" he asks Sam.

*Come with us. Come with us.*

Sam checks his watch again. "I'll come with you guys. Maybe we'll run into them somewhere."

Hurray!

"This'd better not be some kind of trick, Sam Rojas," Lexie says as she pulls keys from her purse.

Sam's mouth drops open and then he laughs.

We cram into the Jeep and, as luck would have it, I end up sitting by him. I couldn't have planned this any better if my life was a movie script. And it feels more and more like one by the minute. I grab the list off the seat and look at the crossed-off items. There are only a couple left worth big points. I stare at item #60, establish two-way communication with an animal.

It gives me a wild idea.

"Hey, let's go to the beach and see if I can communicate with those dolphins. You know, the ones that have been on the news."

There's a gaping silence in the Jeep.

"It's worth five-hundred points. It probably guarantees us that we'll win. It's a good idea. I know I can do it. C'mon."

Tara shakes her head. "I don't know. I think it's too far to the beach." She pouts at me. "Sorry."

Lucas grabs the list from me. "Yeah. It doesn't leave us much time for any of these other things. Sorry."

Everyone stares at me and then Sam pipes up, "I know I'm not on this team, but I think you should do it. Even if you lose, we all win when Jane swims."

Lexie eyes Sam in the rearview mirror and then breaks into a grin. "Damn straight. Who cares if we lose?"

Lucas agrees with Lexie. He almost always does. Willow and Tara shrug.

"Text Irwin." Lexie shoves her phone into Lucas' hand, and he tippy-taps a quick message. Less than a minute later the phone buzzes.

"Irwin wants to see it. He's meeting us at the beach," Lucas says.

Euphoria. I'm thrilled to be cruising toward the swim and right now everything is hysterical. I can't stop myself from laughing.

As I giggle, Sam's phone rings. Alana's name lights up the display.

Sam talks in a super-low voice. I lean forward and whisper in Lexie's ear, "It's Alana." He quickly ends the call and says, "I'm in trouble. She's mad."

"Why?" I ask, giggling despite myself.

"When you were laughing she said, 'I hear Jane Robinson. You're with Jane Robinson. I know her laugh.' So I told her I was riding along with you guys to the beach because you're going to communicate with dolphins and asked if they wanted to pick me up there. Then she said I was cheating on her and hung up."

Is this cheating? Certainly not romantically. But Sam is playing for a different team, so maybe. A leftover laugh pops out even though it's not too funny.

Lucas goes back to playing DJ. He's been at this all night and we've sung a couple oldies, but none of them fall into the anthem definition. Suddenly, he hears one and cranks the volume.

Lexie sings along. "Get your motor runnin'."

I join the other Fallopian Tubes and our volume increases, so by the time we get to the chorus, we're yelling at the top of our lungs, "Like a true nature's child, we were born, born to be wild."

Lucas and Sam must think we're hysterical and maybe a little weird, but they sing and by the end of the song, somebody in a car next to us would have thought we'd all escaped from a mental hospital. The six of us are shrieking the song when it finishes. We all crack up. And add thirty points to our total.

~~~

News of my swim spreads from pod to pod, like a choice fishing spot, and everyone's phones keeping going off. A few of the other teams beat us to the beach—the courtyard pod because for them the hunt was only something to do, and the science lab kids because they're the group that always completes assignments early. Irwin stands off to the side.

Offshore, two dolphins surface and submerge.

"Look! There they are!" a disembodied voice behind me says.

I sleepwalk toward the water. Blurry. Warm.

Sam grabs me by the shoulder. "Wait a minute. I have something for you." He runs toward the Jeep, his feet kicking back at an awkward angle as he moves through the sand. Good thing he's on the swim team instead of track.

But he returns quickly with his drawstring bag, opens it and pulls out a set of goggles that dangle from his hand. He tips my chin up and fits the goggles on me, adjusting the straps like a pro until they're snug. "Push on them, like this." His palms are flat and I copy the motion. He reaches out, wiggles them side to side, and tells me to push again. "It really sucks when you get water in them," he says. "You need to be able to see."

# CHAPTER TWENTY-FIVE

Wading in, the lip of the waves froths at my ankles. The sun is heading down, turning the water to oranges and reds. Deeper and deeper I walk—knees, hips. Feeling anxious. What if the dolphins don't like me as much as I like them? What if the incident when I was five was a fluke—not a dolphin-tail fluke—just unusual?

Oh, well. It's too late to turn back now.

*C'mon, Jane.*

That's not the voice in my head. It's younger and higher. I heard it that night on the shore with Travis. It's them.

The water reaches my shoulders and they're not far away.

*She's coming.*

Either I've lost my mind or I really can hear them. And since I'm not five years old anymore, maybe Desiree's right about the reincarnation thing. There are stranger things in this world. I dive into the oncoming surf.

Swimming now. I've become weightless. All anxiety, all nervousness, all fear, gone. I'm calm and alert. The dolphins are within arm's length. They circle me closer and closer. Concentric.

The largest is named Bella; the other Nica. I don't know how I know this.

Nica swims close. *Look at her. She likes us.*

Bella joins her. *We're going to have fun.*

Tiny currents swirl around us. A small fish swims by in front of me. I hold my arms straight out to the sides and float. The dolphins submerge.

Something big is in the water behind me, unseen. It's Bella. I feel her clicks and whistles telling me, *I'm here.* Desiree would call this "good vibrations."

Suddenly Bella glides by. I lay my hand to her side. It's silky, like rushing water. Then she's gone.

*Come back*, I call.

Bella's back. Then Nica flies by.

Again.

And again, more times than I can count.

Bella dives under. Her silver fluke is the last part to disappear.

Where'd she go?

Nica glides up and elevates half of her body out of the water in front of me. She towers over me. *She'll be back. You're a strange-looking dolphin.*

It's amazing to understand their dolphin language, or maybe I'm hearing their thoughts like Nica just heard mine.

She smiles at me with a gentle, ageless face. *Follow me.* She disappears exactly like Bella.

I press the goggles the way Sam showed me and flipper under. There's silence as large as the ocean itself. Then a sound like a creaking door and *click, click, click*. I exhale a little, and only hear the sound of my bubbles.

Bella swims at me and then elevates to brush the surface. She's created a large ball-sized bubble that she pushes around with her bottlenose, and then taps it to Nica. They bat it back and forth. A game. Finally Nica bites it, creating a million tiny bubbles.

I gulp underwater the last of my air. Surfacing, I gasp and swallow a huge inhale, then re-submerge.

Bella's made another bubble and nudges it to me, but when I try to send it back, it pops. She makes another and this time, with the palm of my hand, I touch it. The bubble wobbles, bouncing through the water until Nica swims up, plants it at the tip of her snout and swims away with it.

Incredible.

I flipper to the surface and tread water. I sense them underneath, a powerful pressure building. Side by side, they break the surface and leap, arc, splash over my head. A face full of water. Salty drops on my lips. Amazing. I must remember to breathe.

Higher!

Bella and Nica are gone, submerged. They leap again.

*Wheeeeeee!* There went Bella.

*Wahooooo!* And that's Nica.

They fly so high. They shine in the last rays of the sun. Bella's belly is impossibly neon pink. Raspberry lipstick pink. Spring impatiens pink. Nica's is a softer pink, like the baby girl shade from Desiree's crib set.

Splash.

Leap, fly, arc. Nica wobbles, a clumsy puppy with paws too big to control. Bella's a well-trained gymnast, her jumps: ten, ten, a perfect ten.

I lift my arms to fly but only float.

At this instant, they're my pod: the dolphins. Bella touches her flipper to my side. *You want to jump?*

*Of course, but I can't,* I tell them.

*You can.* Bella and Nica swim away, and I feel the pressure below the surface again. They place their snouts into the soles of my feet.

Like a hard little fist, they push.

Water rushes around me as we pick up speed. My chest lifts out of the water. I'm one with them as I crest halfway out of the water. The setting sun blinds me. One last push, and I'm flying.

I am Dolphin Girl.

Bella agrees. *You are.*

*You're one of us.* Nica clicks.

My mouth is stretched into the widest grin possible. A dolphin grin, one that never fades.

The two girls circle me again, and Bella spins away and under. Reappearing almost instantly, a huge piece of seaweed dangles from both sides of her snout. She opens her mouth, filled with hundreds of tiny teeth, and I reach in to pluck it out.

Bella chirps, *I love you.*

I let her know, *Me too. I love you.*

She swims forward, and I kiss her. Her snout is hard, like kissing a rubbery elbow. Nica swims to me, and I kiss her too.

There's more love in these dolphin kisses than my human kiss with Travis. I'm totally blissed-out and look at the shore. I see Sam. It doesn't matter if he loves me. It's enough just to love him. I hope we get to kiss someday. I do, I really do.

Nica tells Bella I love Sam.

Bella whistles. *I can tell.*

Nica bumps me. *We have to go now. Are you coming with us to meet the others?*

Bella splashes Nica with water. *That's her pod on land. She can't come.* Bella's older and wiser.

*Yes. They are*, I tell Nica, sad to leave them behind. *But I'm so glad to have met you.*

They hover in front of me. *Bye, Janey.* And then they whirl away so fast I can't follow them even if I wanted.

~~~

Walking out of the surf, I feel gravity. All the kids cluster into their pods, but it's different from the main hall. They seem more—together—mixed in amongst the sand sculptures.

Lexie runs up, throws her arms around me and says, "That was incredible!"

In turn, Willow, Lucas and Tara are lined up behind her. They each give me a hug while Sam stands off to the side.

I take the goggles to him and he bends, kissing the middle of my forehead. He folds me into a hug, rocking back and forth. "That was the best," he whispers.

When he lets go, I shiver, unsure if it's the ocean breeze or Sam's victory hug.

"It was good, huh?" I'm trying to read Sam's expression, staring into his deep brown eyes.

"It was sick." Nigel is sitting on a raggedy blanket right next to me and Sam.

Andre agrees. "Yeah, totally hardcore."

Nigel pushes Andre off the blanket and makes a lame attempt to shake out the sand. He wraps it around me. It smells like sweat and reefer and beach. The sand scratches, but I am warmer with it.

"Thanks," I say.

Sam follows me as I head to a grinning Irwin. Nigel's blanket flows behind me like a queen's robe.

"Fifty points," Irwin says. "That made me happy."

I hug him, and his grin grows impossibly wide. He's wearing a dolphin expression.

"That, too." He takes his clipboard. "Any other points I need to count?" he yells to the teams. Alana, Brendon/Brandon and Karen Perry walk up to our circle.

"I gave her goggles," Sam says. "That's help, right? And Nigel gave her the blanket."

Alana sneers. "That was quite a show." She's baiting me, but I don't take it. "So Irwin, who won?" she asks.

"Jane's team," Irwin says.

I wrap Nigel's blanket tighter around me. "We did?"

"Oh, yeah. I'm just trying to figure out by how much." Irwin's fingers fly over his calculator.

"It doesn't matter," I say.

Irwin stops and takes this corny cup trophy. "The winner of the first annual Western Everglades Scavenger Hunt is The Bohemians." He hands me the cup and I turn it over to Lexie, who screams and does a little booty dance, pumping our trophy over her head. Willow, Tara and Lucas start dancing with her and drag me into the circle.

But getting the cup is not nearly as satisfying as the swim.

Sam grabs my elbow and steers me away from the celebration. "I need to talk to Alana about some stuff, but I wanted to thank you for not leaving me at Wendy's and letting me see you swim and everything."

He hugs me one more time and I don't want to let go, but I do. "Later!" I use a casual voice that doesn't fit with my mood.

Sam walks over to Alana, who smiles up at him.

I head over to my best friend, who's still a maniac boogie machine.

Lexie stops dancing. "You know what Sam did while you swam?"

I shrug.

"He didn't take his eyes off you and didn't say a word until the end when you kissed the dolphins. Then, he whispered, 'lucky dolphin.'" Lexie smiles.

"It doesn't matter."

She looks at me like I've lost my mind. Willow treks toward us through the sand, holding my purse in front of her. "Your phone rang five times while you were out there."

I dig for the phone, find it and flip it open. Five calls, five messages. All from John about thirty minutes ago. I know without listening what they say but play one just to be sure.

"We have to go. Now!" I say to Lexie. "Take me to Memorial Hospital."

*The social group of adult female dolphins is called a matriline, meaning that pods of adult females often contain mothers, daughters, sisters, grandmothers and aunts. These close ties with other female relatives are the most pronounced during the birth of a dolphin calf, when the female relatives assist in bringing the newborn to the surface for its first breath.*

*(Excerpt:* The Magic and Mystery of Dolphins*)*

# CHAPTER TWENTY-SIX

Desiree is *hee, hee, whoo*ing, but no one laughs this time.

She went into labor today, two weeks early. I arrive to the birthing room late, crusted in salt, hair matted. Mom stands next John and they hover over Desiree, who is half-sitting, half-laying in her hospital bed. Although it's only three weeks since I left home Mom looks years older. Worry lines ripple across her face and dark circles are anchored beneath her eyes.

"Jane." Her voice catches and she motions me over to the bed. My throat tightens.

I ease next to her and her hand encircles my shoulders, pulling me in for a squeeze. I want to tell them *I swam with the dolphins,* but don't. The room except for Desiree's breathing is as quiet as a chapel.

Our surroundings are not what I expected. When Desiree had explained birthing rooms to me as "a more natural environment where John, the baby and I can all sleep together," I'd envisioned a hotel room. But the birthing room is a hospital room with makeup. If you put makeup on a guy, it's easy to tell he's still a guy. And even though they've tried to pretty this up, it's still a hospital room. All the equipment and gizmos are a constant reminder of that.

I wonder if this bothers Desiree, but she doesn't seem to notice.

The nurse snaps a glove off and gives Desiree's ankle a gentle pat. "You're coming along fine."

John holds Desiree's hand while she wrings his, clutching it so tightly it's gotta hurt. Eyes worried, he wipes her forehead and whispers something to make her laugh.

Mom hasn't let go of me. Her arm is wrapped around my waist, her hand rests on my Dolphin Girl tattoo. It surprises me that she hasn't scolded me or made a big deal about the fact that I'm wearing only jean shorts, a swimsuit top and flip flops in the hospital, but, well, there's a baby on the way so I guess that's a bigger deal.

As the labor gets harder and harder, it comes to a point where I can't stand to watch Desiree struggle. There's something heavy caught in my chest and throat, like the baby is laying there instead of in its womb.

The nurse says, "Time to push."

Suddenly John leaves Desiree's side and sits next to me on the sofa, head in his hands between his knees. Mom's taken John's place, holding Desiree's hand, and the midwife is positioned to deliver the baby.

I'm an awkward intruder. I don't belong here. If Desiree had not asked me to come, I'd bolt for the waiting room and sit with Dad.

I tap John's leg. "Go to her."

John just shakes his head.

Desiree is gone. It's not her tranquil Madonna face, and it's not the scared expression from earlier. She's totally inside herself.

The nurse comes over to us. "Are you okay?" she asks John.

This is funny because Desiree is the one in pain. Then I think about the finger stick at the pre-natal appointment. How I thought it was a big deal.

I'd let the doctor stick every finger and toe every day for a year if I thought it would ease Desiree's pain. But I know that won't help. It occurs to me this is how John feels. Helpless.

Mom lets Desiree squeeze her hand 'til it turns purple. She whispers near Desiree's ear, "You're doing great. Almost there, honey." Is this my mom?

After midnight, the baby gets closer, and the nurse rubs the top of the baby's head in circular motions to lower her heart rate. It works. On the fetal monitor, you can see the baby calm. It's hard for her, too.

"One more push," the midwife says. And it happens so fast I almost miss the birth. She pops out. Not a pretty sight—all wet and scrunched.

Is she okay?

Seems to be, because everyone is laughing and crying at the same time. The nurse lays the baby on Desiree's belly while John bends over to give them both a kiss.

"Do you want to cut the cord?" The nurse hands a pair of surgical scissors to John. He hesitates and passes them on to me. I never knew he was so squeamish.

I stand over Desiree and the baby, place the cord between the blades of the scissors and squeeze. It's like gristle on a tough steak, rubbery and thick. Even at birth, the cord that binds us to our mothers is powerful.

"I can't do it. I'm not strong enough."

Mom comes over and lays her hand on top of mine. With the added pressure we're able to cut the cord together. We both laugh with relief.

The nurses bundle the baby away to clean, weigh and measure. Her head is enormous, and her legs are peddling away kinda spastically. They're really short compared to her body.

"Is she all right?" I ask Mom.

She's wearing a blissed-out expression. "She's perfect." If anyone would know...

Mom leaves to get Dad and when they return he asks, "Have you decided on a name?"

Desiree looks at John. "We were thinking Lillian Jane. We'd call her Lily—like the flowers Jane's going to paint in the nursery. And 'Jane' is after her godmother." Desiree gives my hand a squeeze.

I look from her to Mom. She beams a smile, and then we're all crying.

The nurse demonstrates how to swaddle Lily. "Babies like this because they still think they're inside. Hold her head close to your heart. The rhythm is comforting." She hands the tightly blanketed bundle to Desiree.

Lily's listened to Desiree's heartbeat for nine months. It must sound a lot like the muffled underwater murmurs Bella and Nica make.

John stands at Desiree's shoulder, stroking her arm. But right now she only has eyes for Lily. She gazes at the baby, smiling and focused, and then hands her to John. As soon as the baby is in his arms, he melts too.

It strikes me that this same scene—or a very similar one—happened when I was born. It's hard to fathom, but I know in the deepest part of me, it's true.

Lily makes a tiny noise that could be fussing. John looks momentarily afraid and tries to hand the baby back to Desiree.

"Do you want to hold her?" Desiree asks me.

I'm stunned by how tiny, light and still the bundle is. Lily's peaceful, sleeping face is framed in black, uneven hair. Her face is still a bit scrunched, but it's no longer scary.

"Who will you be like?" I ask her silently.

Disciplined like Mom, or untamed like Desiree? It's possible she'll have a little of each. *Will you be a little like me? Whatever that means.*

All of a sudden she opens her deep, deep blue eyes and rounds her lips into a perfect little O. She's looking at me, but it's like she can't quite see me.

That's not quite right. She just sees me differently than others do. She sees me through a baby's eyes, and I wonder what that looks like. I'd love to paint it.

*Welcome to the world, sweet baby. Welcome to our pod, Lillian Jane.*

~~~

After the nurses have left and we've all taken turns passing Lily around many, many times, Desiree yawns.

John points to the couch. "Home sweet home. That's where I'll be sleeping."

It hits me hard. I have no way back to their apartment and

even if I did, it would be so lonely there tonight.

Mom slips her arm around me. "Come home, honey?"

Home? It's not really a place anymore.

I nod once, and we stroll out of the room together tossing out, *see you tomorrow* and *bet we sleep better than you*. That kind of stuff.

The car ride is as silent as when we were timing Desiree. At one point, Dad pats Mom's leg and says, "You can relax, Liz."

"I can't relax." She sighs. And there's silence again.

Right before we get to the house, Mom turns around halfway in her seat and whispers, "Can we talk for a minute when we get home?"

Car doors slam, and I feel so awkward. I haven't been here for three weeks, but it feels much longer.

Mom follows me to my room. The first thing I notice is the bed's made, the clothes are all hung. This doesn't surprise me. But what is a shock is how Mom left everything else of mine alone—the mobiles, the bulletin board. It's still my room.

Flipper's tank has been moved to my desk. He swims in little loop-de-loops.

"You fed him."

Mom shakes her head. Her eyes are sparkly and wet. "Your dad. He never missed a day."

I can't believe Dad fed Flipper. Was I wrong about his apathy? I sprinkle a few flakes for my fishy and then face the wall across from my bed to look at the mural.

Ah. Without a doubt, it's the best painting I've ever done. I could tell it was good, but not how much so until I'd been away for a while. Still, I see ways to make it better. Like, I'll paint a bright pink belly for Bella, or I'll paint Nica playing with an underwater bubble. And now, I can paint me.

Mom crumples onto my bed, finally speaking. "Jane, it's beautiful."

What? "You like it?"

"Like it? I love it."

I'm speechless. This isn't what I'd expected. Then I notice all my plastic tubs stacked on the floor in front of it, and there's a tube of midnight blue paint that's been used. Somehow I missed the intricate frame around the mural. I get closer to examine it.

Someone has painted the words "Jane and the dolphins" over and over and over again so that it frames the entire mural. It must say it hundred times, maybe more. The script is neat and delicate. It would've taken forever to paint that.

"You?" I point to the frame.

"Me." Mom smiles and brushes the comforter next to her for me to sit. When I do, she pats my leg. "Honey, I know we're very different people." One tear escapes, and Mom wipes it away. "That's not new." She laughs—an uncomfortable sound, like when you stub your toe and laugh at yourself, even though it hurts like heck. "Lord knows I don't do everything perfectly."

This astounds me more than anything so far.

"I don't know how to start." Mom looks beyond my ceiling for help. "You know about my miscarriages. But you might not know they were hard on me. Especially the second one. After that one, I didn't get out of bed for a month."

Mom's so busy, busy all the time. I can't imagine her just lying in bed. "How far along were you?"

"For two of them. I was barely pregnant. But on the second one, I was five months." Mom rounds her hands in front of her.

It's the stage Desiree was at when she married John. A tear slips onto my cheek.

"Going through that really changed me. Do you know what I mean?"

I manage a nod.

"I used to be freer. Never artistic like you, but not so…controlling." Mom heaves a huge sigh.

I wipe at the tears streaming down my face.

"And you're very sensitive, you know, Jane?"

"I'll work on it," I tell her, crying.

Mom purses her lips, and tears return to her eyes. "No, don't change. It's a nice quality. It's what makes you Jane." She pats her own chest hard. "Now me, I'm good at organizing. That's how I cope. That's all. If I can keep things organized, I feel in control. When life throws chaos at me, it helps me to believe I can count on something."

I never thought of it that way. I always thought it was something she was doing to us, not something for her.

"I always want to fix things for you." Mom takes a deep breath and plunges ahead. "When John got married and was going to have a baby, well, that turned my world upside down." Mom is crying now. "I didn't know what to think or do. Then you moved out and I thought I'd lost you. And I couldn't fix that either." Mom sobs so hard she can't speak.

I reach out and hold her, patting her back. Comforting her. Like she's done for me so many, many times.

"It's okay," I murmur in rhythm with each pat. "The baby's fine. John's fine. Desiree's fine. We're fine. Everything's going to be fine."

# CHAPTER TWENTY-SEVEN

Sam towers over the water fountain on Monday morning after the Scavenger Hunt. My face cracks into a grin and I hurry to him, not caring that I've lost any chance to appear aloof. He bends and gives me a peck on my cheek.

Lexie's brought the trophy to school. She directs the stream of water from the fountain into it and we pass it from person to person. After Sam drinks, he grabs my hand and pulls me through the main hall. At first I think he's taking me to the trophy case, but we cruise by. Alana's got her back to us and doesn't bother to look when Ashley whispers in her ear.

I have no idea where Sam's headed. We pass the science lab crowd. I wave at Brenden/Brandon—will I ever remember his name? As we breeze through the exit, we pass the courtyard crowd, and Nigel salutes.

"Where are we going?" I ask.

"Almost there."

On Sunday I hoped Sam would call and explain what had happened when he talked with Alana. I so didn't love the suspense. But he never did. To distract me, I played with the daisy for my mobile. *He loves me. He loves me not.*

I couldn't remember my odds on this, so I pulled up the bookmark on daisies and this time read the entry on Fibonacci numbers. It's a mathematical sequence where you add every number to the prior one so it goes like this 1, 1, 2, 3, 5, 8, 13. It's a cool pattern, but that's not the amazing part. This is: in nature, in everything really, this sequence is pleasing to people. It's in pineapples and turtles and trees and music and art and—daisies.

I don't understand why they don't teach this kind of math instead of the quadratic formula. There's order in the universe. Not organization created by us, like Mom and her lists, but an underlying plan. Isn't that important to know?

So I try to let this reassure me as Sam guides me to a spot under the big tree in front of the school. He plops his backpack onto the ground and sits, resting against it. I do the same.

"Time to talk about everything," Sam says.

Oh, God, no. I can't believe he's going to do this now. Couldn't he have just said everything he needed to say on the phone?

Then I think three random thoughts:

The dolphins are in my pod.

He's not a trophy.

Order in the universe.

These thoughts fill me with courage. I take a deep breath. "All right."

Sam takes a deep breath too and plunges ahead. "When I first met you, I thought you were a little—don't take this in the wrong way—different."

I yank grass from the ground.

"But I'm really glad we got put into the freshman lunch hour, because otherwise I wouldn't have gotten to know you."

Just like I thought. Taking a blade of grass, I tear it down the middle.

"I looked forward to our lunches. I liked that you were different than the girls I usually hang around. You're not so into clothes, shopping and yourself."

Blades of grass are piling up in front of me from all the tugging. A weird thought runs through my head, *Desiree would disapprove of me killing all this grass.*

"I'd told Travis I wanted to ask you to the Snow Ball, but Chase was trying to convince me to ask Alana because that's what Ashley wanted."

I can't believe he was going to ask me. I can't believe my intuition was right. "So what happened that day in the parking lot?"

"I still don't know." Sam throws his hands in the air. "I

guess Alana and Ashley set it up. Then, after I fixed you up with Travis, I couldn't believe he changed the plans."

I stop uprooting grass and rest my elbows on my knees, my fists propping my chin. "Maybe he was feeling that everyone liked you better. He said something about that to me."

"He did?" Understanding dawns Sam's eyes. "I never realized."

Suddenly I get how Travis feels. Yeah, he might be a dawg. And annoying. A complete a-hole at times. But it's hard to always feel inferior to a friend. Look at me and Alana. And she's an ex-bestie. "Maybe he felt like you'd forced him to take me. I mean, he wanted to be with Alana, right?"

"Maybe—but I was trying to help him be with Alana and when we didn't go to the same restaurant, when I heard you hooked up with Travis, I…" Sam stops.

I want to fill in the emptiness with questions. Felt confused? Felt relief?

He fills in. "Got pissed."

Oh yeah. That's right.

"So, I started dating Alana. And you know the rest."

I remind myself about the swim. About the feeling with the dolphins. Having half of what you want is better than having nothing. "So, go ahead," I say. "What's the rest?"

Sam's perplexed. "You were right. I stayed with Alana because, because it's what everyone else wanted. It was easier. I broke up with her after The Hunt."

My eyes open so wide I think they must they must resemble Irwin's, magnified behind his smudged glasses.

"I like someone else." Sam rests his hand on my knee. "I like this girl who draws and paints, likes corny jokes and thinks she's reincarnated from a dolphin." Sam leans forward, so close he's an inch from my face. "Can I buy you a tuna sandwich at lunch?" he asks.

I giggle. "Yes."

He doesn't back away. "Will you take me to the preserve after school?"

I stop giggling and look at his mouth. He's got his tongue against the chipped tooth again, waiting for my answer. I look into his deep brown eyes. "Plan on it."

~~~

Sam's hand engulfs mine as we walk three blocks to the preserve in silence. In my case, it's anticipation. I've wanted to take him to the preserve forever. But Sam's not usually quiet, and I don't know why all of a sudden today he is. Maybe he's run out of things to say?

Finally I ask, "Did you see Alana today?"

"I talked to her in the hall for a minute."

I don't want to ask a follow-up question so I just peek at

Sam's profile.

"I don't know. She's still acting mad, but to be honest, I think she's pretending. I don't think it bothered her much."

I always thought she liked the idea of Sam—the right guy, the right group—more than she actually liked him. But I still wondered what he meant.

"She said, 'It's good I broke up with you and I hope you don't do something pathetically stupid, like picking a rebound chick, especially one outside of our crowd. That would make you look totally desperate.'"

"What'd you say?"

"I reminded her we broke up because she felt I was cheating, so why did she care? Also, I told her it wouldn't bother me if she found another guy right away. That I hoped she'd find the right person for her."

Alana and I will never be good friends again, but I do hope she finds the right guy. "For Travis to care about any one girl is so different, but he does."

"I know, and she doesn't plan on sitting at home. That's why I don't think she's too upset."

"Are you?"

"Am I what?"

"Upset."

"Well it wasn't fun to break up with her, but I'm glad that's behind me."

When we get close to the entrance, I notice the parking lot, which is really only five or six spaces for visitors. It's empty, and it hits me—Sam and I are alone. Totally alone. We've never been alone before.

Oh sure, we've come close, like lunches together. Except there are about three-hundred kids around us in the café. Or when we danced at the Winter Ball, I felt like I was alone with him, but still we were surrounded by classmates. Even the time when we studied *Romeo and Juliet*, John and Desiree were in the next room.

Sam's thinking is in sync with mine because he says, "There's no one else here."

"It's so peaceful. That's why I love it."

I steer Sam over the wooden walkways, raised above the water and saw grass, to my favorite spot at the edge of the dock. We sit in the shade of a small roof and dangle our legs above the water, watching fairy tale ducks swim around.

You'd think being alone with Sam, I'd feel anxious, but I don't. Not in the least. I rest my head on his shoulder and he puts his hand on the ground behind my back, letting me use his arm for support.

"Sometimes I imagine that dolphins would swim up to me." I point to a spot in front of us. "Right there."

Sam kisses me on the temple, hitting the same spot he did when we rehearsed *Romeo and Juliet*. I love it when he does this, but I want a real one.

I turn my head toward him and bite my lower lip.

Sam gets the hint. He looks in my eyes and lowers his head. I catch my breath. There's an enormous lump in my throat. His fingertips graze my cheeks. His lips are soft and warm. I kiss him back and then I'm floating, drifting away on the current of Sam.

~~~

I don't know how long we kissed, only that the sun had moved enough we no longer were shaded by the roof.

Kissing Sam is nothing like kissing Travis. Travis had lots of moves that would have earned him extra points for technical difficulty if he was a diver. A reverse, double-twisting pike, that sort of thing. Sam's kisses are simple, but I feel each from my lips to the tips of my pinky toes.

"I guess we'd better go," I say, my eyes only half open.

Sam kisses me one more time and stands, offering his hand to help me up. "C'mon, Dolphin Girl."

He holds my backpack for me to slip my arms through, and I hand his to him. This is exactly what I had in mind last December, before the parking lot trap. It's strange how months after I'd planned, it happened almost like I'd dreamed with one big difference.

Kissing Sam was even better than I'd imagined.

# EPILOGUE

I complete the pink baby bottle for my mobile, the last trinket to fasten to it. Desiree quipped I should have done a breast, since she doesn't advocate bottle-feeding. But I explained the bottle only symbolizes the baby, not her preferred feeding method.

Standing on my desk chair, I hang the mobile and softly tap each item: a mini-sized Dolphin Girl costume, a daisy, an ice skate, a peanut, William Shakespeare's head, a large piece of seaweed, a mini scavenger hunt trophy and the baby bottle.

This has been an eventful year.

Back in October I yearned for freedom, only to realize, it all comes down to one word, one thought.

Choice.

And I'd been making choices, some good and some not, all year long.

Choosing when to rebel and who to befriend. Choosing to

date and kiss a boy I didn't even like. Choosing to run away, to come home, to forgive.

What have I picked for today?

To finish my mobile, and paint the garden mural in Lily's nursery, and go to the movies with Sam tonight. And help Mom around the house.

Things are not perfect between Mom and I, but nothing ever is. I've stopped worrying about the ideal—my version of a perfect mom or being her perfect daughter.

Mom's trying to be more relaxed and I'm trying to be more organized. Because life is a combination of chaos and order. In a way, it's like dolphins. Above the surface there might be heart-stopping excitement with energetic leaps, but underneath there's quiet beauty and grace.

Maybe I was a dolphin in a previous life, or maybe I'll be one in the future, but in this one—the one that counts—I'm human. I've realized God does not make mistakes, like I once thought.

Everyone else does. Sam, John, Desiree, even Mom. They all make mistakes.

And because I'm human, so do I.

# EXTRAS

Under Jane's bed, in the bottom of her duffle bag are three lists. Two are from the day she ran away from home: the list of what's wrong with her life and the list her mom had already hung on the fridge. The third is the official list for The Hunt.

I think what Jane would tell us about these lists, is that in photography when you zoom in on something, that's when you can pick out seemingly insignificant differences.

Life isn't like that.

Being close makes it harder.

If you compare Jane's list and her mom's list to the one from The Hunt, you'll see how her life had shifted. It might not have been a seismic shift, but as it turned out that didn't matter.

**To Do Today 02/11**

1. Weed the planters at the back of the house. Be sure to do a good job around the base of the hedges.
2. Dust blinds and ceiling fans (both sides!!!!!)
3. Scrub upstairs bathroom. Mop the floor twice – fresh water on the second mop! Also, I bought a new mop it's in the laundry room. Please use it. Vacuum area rugs and stairs.
4. Enchiladas 350 degree oven @ 5:10 pm
5. Fold clothes in dryer. Wash a load of bath towels

Thanks, Honey! XO, Mom

## MY LIFE:

1. BYE-BYE DOLPHIN SWIM.
2. CAN'T HANG OUT WITH LEXIE.
3. TRAVIS TOOK ME TO RODEO BOB'S.
4. THEN LIED ABOUT THE BEACH.
5. AND I KISSED HIM.
6. SAM AND ALANA ARE A COUPLE.
7. IRWIN'S NOT SPEAKING TO ME.
8. I NEVER SEE JOHN ANY MORE.
9. MOM DOESN'T WANT ME TO BE THE GODMOTHER.
10. MOM'S LISTS MAKE ME NUTTY.

Shel Delisle

# 1st Annual WEHS Scavenger Hunt

The hunt will begin in the Western Everglades High School parking lot at 2 pm sharp. You are expected to check in with the judge at the times and locations below.

First check-in: The Mall – south entrance 3:30pm
Second check-in: Coldstone 5:00 pm
Final check in: Western Everglades High 7:00 pm

The items included on this list require different skills: intelligence, physical prowess, creativity, organization and humor. This will ensure that the talents of all teams are used.

You have five hours to complete this contest. Proof of items can be sent via cell phone or digitally recorded or brought to the judges. DO NOT BREAK THE LAW OR HARM ANYONE OR THEIR PROPERTY!!!!!! Have Fun.

1. Get an eye exam and ask for extra credit. (30 pts.)
2. Do "something" for a Klondike Bar. (10-50 pts. based on originality)
3. Post 'Wanted" posters of a heinous criminal around town. (5 pts./per poster)
4. Find someone who can lick their elbow. (50 pts.)
5. Locate Area 51. (51 pts.)
6. Purchase condoms in every color of the rainbow. (10 pts./color)
7. Do something wild and out of control. (15 pts.)
8. Have an "Herbal Essence Experience" using peanut butter. (15 pts.)
9. Bribe a judge. (pts. vary)
10. Lose your innocence. (10 pts.)
11. Re-locate your lost innocence. (30 pts.)

12. Dress in a costume and run through the mall. (30 pts.)
13. Collect pens, stationery or other free giveaways from local businesses. (10pts. for each unique item, max 100 pts.)
14. Ask information to connect you to the Dalai Lama. (10 pts.)
15. Find a functioning 8-track player. (50 pts.)
16. Purchase exactly $.50 of gasoline. (20 pts. Proof of purchase required.)
17. Put your foot in your mouth. (15 pts.)
18. Scare the crap out of someone. (5pts. Bonus for same thing literally 100 pts.)
19. Capture a Shriner and bring him to HQ. (100 pts.)
20. Calculate the most cost effective way of purchasing 10,000 calories at McDonalds and buy it. (25 pts. consume it – 75 pts.)
21. Have a team member wear excessive make-up. (10 pts. Bonus if member is male 20 pts.)
22. Have a hair-raising experience. (with mousse or gel 10 pts, without styling aids 40 pts.)
23. Pet a cow. (50 pts.)
24. Fight "Corporate America" (50 to 100 pts. Judge's discretion.)
25. Find a Rubik's Cube. (10 pts. Solve it in front of the judge 40 pts.)
26. Call a phone number from a bathroom wall. (10 pts. Bonus 10 pts. for each minute of conversation, max 50 pts.)
27. Run a team member's underwear up the flagpole. (20 – 50 pts. Judge's discretion.)
28. Address me as Tad. (10 pts.)
29. Perform a rock version of a favorite childhood song. (20 pts.)
30. Make me happy. (50 pts.)
31. Create a lengthy secret handshake. (10 pts. per minute, 30 pts. max.)

32. Find a street with the same name as someone on your team. (20 pts.)
33. Read my mind. Figure out what was I thinking when I wrote this item. (50 pts.)
34. Make chicken soup for the soul using shredded pages from the book as noodles. (50 pts.)
35. Locate a rock anthem on the radio. This song must be more than 10 years old. (10pts. With a 20pt. bonus if the team can sing along.)
36. Have another team help you with something. (40 pts.)
37. Find Waldo. (10 pts.)
38. Calculate a Barbie dolls measurements as if she were a real person. (25 pts.)
39. Turn on your car. (10 pts. Bonus 20 pts. if it turns you on)
40. Find currencies from as many different countries as possible. (10 pts. per country)
41. Calculate the number of minutes you have to complete each item on the hunt if your team could do every item. (10 pts.)
42. Create a legally binding contract for something trivial. (15 pts.)
43. Translate fifteen items from this document into Latin or the entire document (including rules) into Pig Latin. (30 pts.)
44. Find your inner child and then punish it. (20 pts.)
45. Create a "cheer' for the hunt. (15 pts., 30 pts. Bonus for making a pyramid.)
46. Take a pregnancy test. (15 pts. 100 pt. bonus for "positive" result if taken by a male team member)
47. Collect sauce packets from Wendy's. (1 pt. each, 5 points for each packet consumed, max 100 pts.)
48. Re-create a famous building, monument or landmark from sand. (25 pts.)
49. Bring a cup from Coldstone to the judge. (30 pts.)
50. Do something amok, no running allowed. (15 pts.)

**Bonus Items:**
51. Find the cure for cancer. (500 pts.)
52. Speak to the Dalai Lama. (500 pts.)
53. Establish two-way communication with an animal. (500 pts.)

## The Judge:  Irwin 'Tad' Sanders
## Teams:

### The Bohemians
Lexington Murphy
Jane Robinson
Lucas Parra
Angeline Bertolli
Tara Weiss

### The Dudes
Nigel Chang
Andre LaBelle
Justin Dunleavy
Richie Gonzalez

### The Champs
Sam Rojas
Alana Atwood
Ashley Grant
Travis Thomlinson
Chase Nichols

### Maniac Brainiacs
Brendon Hoth
Derek Mee
Grace Chin
Rodney Whipple

### The Adventurers
Jordan Wilson
Karen Perry
Christina Hernandez
Sachi Patel

# ACKNOWLEDGMENTS

Huge thanks are owed to many people for helping me make this book a reality.

To my husband and children—Ken, Matt, Cam and Ryan—I owe you guys a lot for putting up with all the times I neglected my real job. Thank you.

To the rest of my large and supportive family: Mom, Dad, Shari, Gary, Muriel, Steph, Eric, Sandy, Brian, Josh, Zack, Sarah, Judy, Ev and Andy. Thank you for giving me ideas or just listening to me blab about writing and books for years and years.

For the two writer peeps who influenced my writing more than anyone else. Thanks to mentor/teacher/friend Joyce Sweeney, who always pushed, prodded or dragged me along a path to better writing. And special thanks to my writing sister Kerry O'Malley Cerra, who has been at my side for the entire journey, providing emotional support and giving advice on all kinds of important details from good restaurants to how to phrase *everything* to character names to which top looks cuter. She even tricked me into seeing these acknowledgments in advance. So I had to change them-ha! Thank you, Kerry and Joyce.

Thank you to two important early readers of the manuscript: Christina Diaz Gonzalez, who made excellent suggestions for adding depth to the characters and Sarah Davies for kind, thoughtful editorial guidance that focused and transformed the story.

Special thanks to my editor Rhonda Stapleton, my cover artist Matt Delisle, my fine-tooth comb proofreader Kristina Miranda and my e-book formatter Guido Henkel. I couldn't ask for a better publication team!

Thank you to Dolphins Plus for a wonderful swim and to Tricadecathlonomania for the scavenger hunt inspiration.

I'm also very grateful for the writing community that has provided all kinds of support over the years. Thanks to Doran Cirrone and Alex Flinn who shaped the story (and my writing future!) at some of my first SCBWI conferences. Also thanks for my Wednesday group critique partners who influenced portions of the story as it evolved from week to week and year to year—Danielle Joseph, Adrienne Silver, Linda Rodriguez Bernfeld, Mindy Dolandis, Mindy Weiss, Flora Doone, Janeen Mason, Debbi Reed Fischer and Shari Winston. Thanks to all the Whatcha' Reading Now? peeps who have shared so many busy, fun, hard-working times. The community we have built together is awesome.

There are many, many others who have advised me through the years. All of the comments—both good and bad—have shaped me. I'm very grateful for all the feedback.

And finally, thanks to my brilliant Panera posse: Kerry O'Malley Cerra, Jill MacKenzie, Meredith McCardle, and Kristina Miranda, who have helped me in so many ways during the last leg of this journey. I couldn't have done this without your encouragement and support. Shine on, girls.

# Dolphin Girl

# ABOUT THE AUTHOR

**SHEL DELISLE** swam with the dolphins once upon a time. While it was an incredible experience, sadly, the dolphins didn't speak to her. Even though she lives in Florida with her hubby and three boys, she doesn't spend as much time as she would like in the water. Most days she writes fiction or works on the kid-lit community website, www.whatchareadingnow.com, that she founded with two other writer friends.

You can also visit her at http://sheldelisle.wordpress.com.